Fantasy & More
COLLECTED
ISSUE ONE

Fantasy & More

COLLECTED
ISSUE ONE

William J. Seymour

B

FANTASY & MORE: Collected Volume One is a work of fiction. Names, places, and incidents either are a product of the author's imagination or are used fictitiously.

A Book Furnace Publications Book

ISBN: 978-1-943266-13-5

Cover Design: Book Furnace Publications

Cover Image: ID# 12475790 © Rangpl | Dreamstime.com

For Those Who Love Stories As Much As I Do

Contents

Introduction

In today's world, who is to say that an idea is too crazy? The fact that someone sits in a room, in front of a computer, uses their imagination to put little pieces of code on the screen, and then that code is purchased by another person for entertainment should be signs that the world itself can be thought of as crazy.

But what if that isn't exactly correct either? Maybe those little pieces of code that have found a way to enlighten and bring people to worlds of imaginable greatness for years upon years isn't crazy, but a magic that is real. Like the flaming sword that stabs into the heart of the dragon that has ravaged the lands for generations, or the kiss from a prince that finally breaks the princess' curse, this magic is as real as we want it to be.

The magic that can bring tears to your eyes, set your heart racing, and your butt ever closer to the edge of your seat.

You know what I speak of. Those times when the palms of your hands are sweaty and time itself leaves you as you enter that space in between where nothing else matters but you and the end of the story.

That space, that special time, is what this project is all about. Stories and the fun I hope they bring to those who sit and read these little bits of code. Each and every story is crafted with the idea of letting a little bit of myself have fun on the page with the hopes that you will find me there and join on the journey. Fantasy & More: Collected is my way of doing just that.

A collection of tales that can bring you to the edge of your seat with epic battles and send your heart racing with danger that won't go away until the very last word. Maybe it will be a mystery that leaves you wondering who did it, and sometimes the bigger question of why?

There won't be any telling what comes your way. How do I know that? I don't even know what is going to find its way into each book. I have no intention of bringing anything but fun and excitement to the page. Maybe it's a post-apocalyptic story at first, and then a fairytale love story bringing you across the fields of a world full of wonder and magic at the end. Who knows? I don't.

I hope you find yourself able to join me though. There will be fun to be had by all. I know I'll have a blast writing it, and I hope you have just as much reading it.

Enjoy your time by my side and enjoy Issue One. A collection of stories old and new. They are only the beginning of what I know will be a grand adventure.

Thankful for what is to come,

William "Roh" Seymour

Black Gold

By
William J. Seymour
©2021

Tobias and his brother have hit the jackpot. After a lifetime of living under their family's shadow of being failures, their luck has finally turned around. They've struck it rich.
Filthy Rich.
Too bad good luck has a way of quickly turning back around.
Black Gold, where your dreams can become nightmares.

At first, we thought the black liquid was oil, that we'd struck it rich and that we'd be able to retire and live in leisure. We actually started writing down all the ways we'd spend the money. Our first choice was to buy some island out in the Caribbean. Live a life in the warm sun, surrounded by half-naked women with a penchant for serving drinks and a strong hatred for clothing. A place that had no use for dust and dirt. Large machinery and too many rules. A paradise waiting for us to come in and live like kings.

Of course, if an island wasn't available, we'd buy at least a small castle or two. Rooms full of servants and maids. Bring in all the celebrities we could think of. Maybe even some royalty. Make them all sleep in the lower quarters. Leaving us with the upper tower overlooking everything that was ours. I can already hear the seagulls calling as the waves crash against the coast. Can you?

Oh, what would it be like to marry a princess? Maybe even two princesses?

I could tell a thought or two of similar design had crossed my brother's mind as well. That shit-eating grin of his hadn't faded since the moment that glorious black gold started spewing high into the air. He's never been much for hiding anything. Mother always said he wore his heart on his sleeve. The real emotional type. First to get sad or angry. Run in when a fight starts and last to give up when you're way past the point of losing. Real stickler for those things he is. It's why he has the scars on his cheeks and the eyes that for some reason women love. I hate him sometimes for that. I never tell him, but it's there. I'm man enough to admit that.

But things were going to change now. Once and for all as the fountain of treasure lifted into the air and crested into the most beautiful wave ever seen on the face of this planet told us so. Heaven on Earth. That's what it was. The answers to all our prayers. No more work. No shitty jobs telling us to get our asses moving or we'll be seeing a pink slip slap us across the face faster than a feral cat high on catnip. Life was going to be easy from this day forward. Not a care in this fucking world. I'm telling you what, we had it all planned out. Even if we weren't going to be able to spend it all, we were going to give it one hell of a shot.

Then it all went bad.

Real fucking bad.

Like end of the world shit here. Not the kind where you call Bruce Willis and send him to the fucking moon bad. I'm talking Death Star, and everything is blown to hell and back bad.

Let me tell you how it all went down. The sun was barely beneath the corn when it all started. A tiny sliver of red above the horizon to the west. One of those perfect sunsets where you want to curl up with a cutie from the drive-in on the other side of town and just forget about the movie all together. It couldn't have been a more picture-perfect end to the greatest day of our lives, but I didn't expect it to actually be our last.

I'm not sure of the exact moment everything changed, but I'm pretty sure when it did, we could never have prepared for what was ahead of us.

***

"Sure, is one hell of sight isn't it," Tobias said.

His smile stretched from one greasy cheek to the other, long streaks of oil marking where he wiped his dirty, sweaty hands across the top of his forehead. His silver eyes danced in the fading sun and for what it was worth, I had never seen him happier.

Everything smelled of oil. It was in the air, on the ground, on our skin, and in our mouths. It was the grandest thing I had ever known. A mix of toxic fumes getting me high and the pure joy knowing that there was no reason for me to ever come down to earth again.

"It sure is fucking beautiful. Ol'grand-pappy's land finally useful for something. Ya remember those stories he used to tell us? How there was oil trapped under this ground. Enough to make us all rich," I said as I leaned back in my chair.

The metal bars where the damn thing would fold always melded well with my ass, but that evening it was nothing more than a pain in the you know what. Maybe it was because I knew I no longer had to worry about replacing it. Money was no object. I could afford a million of these specials from Walmart. But tonight, there wasn't enough beers in the world that would make it any more comfortable.

"Yeah, I remember what he said. Grandma and her crazy sticks. Certain she could find us the oil," Tobias answered with a chuckle. Pulling off his hat he let the long curly locks of his hair fall around his face, the dirty blond strands now as dark and oily black as the skin on his hands, the ground at our feet, and the table between us. "Why do you think we didn't find it until now?"

"Hell, if I should know. Does it matter? Poor bastards, may God bless their souls, didn't look in the correct spot that's all," I said.

Deep down I did feel bad. My grandfather had spent more than forty years drilling out here in the deadpans of South Dakota to find nothing more than a bitter wife, a dead ranch, and some unreliable grandsons.

But not anymore. This night, Tobias and Leonard Pacupsy were far more than failed oil drillers and worthless farm hands. No matter what those bas-tards back in Sioux City said, after this evening, we were going to be rich.

Filthy fucking rich!

"So…who do we call first?" Tobias asked.

To be honest I hadn't thought about it that much yet. Too busy dreaming of the hula girls and princesses to even bother. The waving short skirts. Bodices tied way too tight and begging for me to tear them apart. Why the hell would I be thinking about who to call? Looking up as the sky finished its transition from a cobalt blue to the endless Milky Way, the geyser of black freedom continued to coat everything in a hundred-foot circle. The realization that I didn't exactly know what the next step was hit me like a shot to the gut which I quickly passed away with another warm belch of beer that was running out way too fast.

"Call the damn oil company, that's who we call. Tell them we have enough barrels to sell to keep them in business for a hundred years! Fucking liberal crybabies and their electric cars. Oil is where it really is. Good old fucking slippery oil. That's what God put it on this earth for, little brother. For us to find and burn in the biggest damn truck we can buy," I said before slapping him across the shoulder.

He nodded and went back to watching as the spray continued like a soft rain.

I'm not sure if it was the beers, the fumes, or just not really caring what my little brother was doing, but I didn't notice when his attention had tilted from where the oil pointed in our direction of opportunity, up and far away from this hell hole in the middle of South

Dakota, but down to the ground. It was a funny place to be looking at. Nothing more than a dark rotating pool split down the center by a crack that looked more like a lightning bolt cut through the soil.

"What's up, Tobi? It looks like you've seen a ghost."

And it had. Beneath the filth and oil across his skin, my brother is normally darker skinned than me, having inherited our father's tanned complexion. I, of course, take more after our mother, but given enough sun, it's hard to deny the family resemblance. Except I'm only two years older and half bald and that bastard could grow a ponytail in a month. At this moment though, he was paler than a knocked up teenage high school girl's wedding dress.

"Do you see that?" he asked as he lifted himself half-way off of his lawn chair.

It was getting so dark, I'm pretty sure I couldn't have seen a Ford Bronco until it was practically running me over, but I tried anyway.

At first there was nothing. Long shadows cast by lights burning on the back porch and silver streams reflecting off the streams of oil as it shot into the air. The horizon barely extended beyond the yard we were sitting in. Thick and musky, the fog rolling off the fountain made it hard to see in what little light we had, but now it had grown so bad the world was nothing more than the oil and our back porch.

How did I not notice it before?

God, I hate closed in places. I shook off the feeling and reached for another beer, but the cooler was empty.

"There is nothing but oil and the path to easy street, Tobi. How about you and I get inside where the air is cleaner, and we get a few more cold ones before calling someone to help clean this shit up?"

"Something is out there," he replied.

White knuckling the small card table between us, I probably couldn't have moved the thing if I hauled off and kicked it.

"Yeah, a million gallons of liquid gold is out there. Now just shut up and let's get inside before these fumes make you start seeing anything else."

I pushed away, damn near tipping myself over, and started to lift myself from the seat. Normally not exactly a feat of strength, but that is some mix, oil fumes and beer. Made everything feel like a hundred pounds. Arms, legs, even my shoes were practically rooted to the dirt.

"No, wait. I see something," Tobias insisted.

With a sigh I looked again. Not really out of caring or concern, more like annoyance.

"Just give it a bre…" I started.

The words lost all meaning and soon tasted as sour as a ruined melon still stuck between my teeth from dinner.

Down at the base of the oil plume, where the crack in the earth zigged and zagged itself away from the drill that tipped over in the eruption, we watched as the ground began to pull itself apart.

Slowly, but with the horrific sound of something big being ripped apart painfully inch by inch, we watched as the opening spread and swallowed bits and pieces of trash we hadn't bothered to pick up since the find. Then, accompanied by the screech of metal being torn apart bolt by bolt, the whole drill was dropped in. More oil erupted in an uncontrollable burst. The warm liquid coated everything to the point it rained on us with its nasty touch from easily two hundred feet away.

I'd be lying if I didn't say I wet myself right then and there. It wasn't the oil that scared me. I'd never seen so much in my life and part of me did actually wonder if we'd made a mistake drilling a hole down to a reserve so deep we might flood the whole world itself, but it was what came after.

Thick and wet. Glistening like a fresh fish pulled straight from the river, but with arms as thick as a bull itself, the fucking devil itself reached up from inside that hole. The ground continued to split as it gave birth to the demon. Mucus dripping with oil and a body rippling with corded muscle and pure malice, the thing wrenched itself from the ground.

I wanted to run I tell you. Every part of me screamed to get the hell out of there and screw the cabana girls and the high-maintenance princesses with their fucking castles. But I couldn't.

Like a fly stuck in glue I watched as that monster set itself free and stretched as if cramped and finally able to extend itself. Fingers with claws like an eagle's talons, the beast was easily twenty feet tall.

Maybe even thirty, but who the hell am I to judge? It could have been fifty and it wouldn't have mattered.

Scared with burn marks of white forming a map across its body, the giant was a linebacker made of horror. Its clawed feet dug into the ground as it settled on our back yard, it's lower jaw gapping as it split into two forked halves before it roared into the night a sound so horrifying, I still can't sleep more than an hour without being piss poor drunk.

Like a thousand souls crying at once, it raged in triumph now that it had been released. Oil slickened its torso and the red fires of its eyes swept all around. At first, I was certain it would squash us in a second.

Two tiny humans hardly larger than its fucking toes, but in the darkness, we must have been nothing more than ants. Eyes glaring, it watched the horizon like a hawk. Flat face unmoving, nostrils flaring, and those demon eyes searching.

For what? I'm not sure. Maybe some hero to come challenge it, but I wasn't going to be the one to ask. Of course, neither was I going to admit to being there if I could possibly slip away unnoticed, but that was a pipedream that ended with the idiotic shout of Tobias.

"You will never take this world without a fight!" he screamed.

I was at a loss for words. Shock, exhaustion, intoxication. I'm not sure which, but there was nothing I could do to stop him.

Shoving himself away from our little unnoticed haven, I watched as he charged the beast. I wanted to scream, yell in protest anything that would possibly stop the damn fool, but it would have been no good.

Hand raised over his head, father's knife held out and at the ready, I watched as he drove himself headfirst through the slick pool of oil and wet grass. I was shocked, scared, stunned, and dumbfounded at the same time.

Motionless, I watched as my brother closed the distance between us and certain death in what felt like an hour but was nothing more than a few heartbeats at best.

As I would have expected, the beast never even registered Tobias until the knife sank into the creature's calf. How deep it actually sliced into that dark flesh and miles of muscle beneath I will never be able to tell, but the look on those eyes.

The eternal flames of hell regarded my brother with a mix of anger and astonishment I never would have thought possible on a creature from the pits of the underworld. It tilted its head to the side, almost in confusion as it regarded Tobias and what he had done.

I always thought myself a learned man of the good book, having regularly found myself in pews at church at least twice a month for the last month or two, but I swear to all that is holy that thing actually stopped and considered its reaction to being stuck by a knife better suited for cutting tomatoes from the stalk than it is downing the spawns of Satan himself.

Now no one can call my brother a smart man. Many have called him an attractive man, but never the sharpest tool in the shed. Standing there looking the devil himself face to face, I'll say at that moment he was the bravest man who ever walked this earth.

For a split second, I thought somewhere deep down inside there was a chance this could all be a dream. One horrible fucking nightmare where I had to realize that for once in my life, I would have to admit there was more to my brother than I had ever given him credit for.

Too bad it was not that evening. With a roar that would make a monster movie proud the behemoth roared and snapped its leg back.

I tried to scream.

"Run away you fucking idiot!" Were the words I wanted to say but the strength failed me.

I watched as a foot larger than our mother's Buick kicked forward and hit Tobias square across pretty much every part of his body. Like a rock thrown by a child at a pile of sticks, I watched as my brother's body crashed through walls of wood and glass.

The sound was wet and sickening. I'm not sure if that is where I puked or later, but breath was very hard to find. Sinking to my knees I watched as the roof of our house caved into the hole Tobias created as he rocketed though the living room.

Part of me wanted to call out to him. Ask him if he was OK and if he could hear me, but at that moment I had a million tons of other problems. Small and unworthy of notice as I was, the little stick Tobias had given the monster was another reason to hate humans on top of what it was already born with. And I was the only one for miles.

With a glare of pure hatred, the monster had now found me. Dark poison dripped from its pointed fangs, and I lost count of how many rows waited for me inside that mouth, somewhere around half a dozen.

It gave me something between a smile and a look of pure hatred that was confusing and terrifying at the same time. Cold dread and ice ran down my spine as I looked for help.

Screams would be no good. My words were

swallowed beneath the howl it roared and the rain of oil made everything slippery. In a single step it closed the distance between us.

Now, I don't count myself a coward, but I reckon anyone in my situation could hardly do any better. The claws of the damn thing smashed that little table of ours in a single motion. The legs bent and the top snapped like kindling.

To be honest it was the grace of God I didn't go down with it as I tried to run away. As slick as a trout fresh out of the water, my boots fell out from under me, and I slid as that damn monster took a swing.

Claws raked through the ground sending a shower of mud high into the air and then all over me. Damn stuff stank of oil and beer as I crawled away.

I'm guessing that between everything that was covering me, it had a hard time keeping my tiny person in its sights. Three more times it tried to grab me. Each time it brought me back to my old high school football days. Back when I used to be known as Slippery Lenny. Linebackers couldn't catch me and when they did, they couldn't keep a finger on me for more than a second.

I rekindled some of that here. Bobbing and weaving. Something like the great Mohammed Ali. A butterfly would have been jealous of the way I zigged, and I zagged across that field.

When I wasn't spinning and making a fool of that monster, I was swimming like a prize-winning fish through that pond of oil. With each miss that demon grew angrier. It roared in frustration, its claws taking holes the size of a car right out of the earth each time it missed me.

I tried to make my way to the house. Maybe, just maybe Tobias would be all right inside. Man has a thick skull after all. Takes more than a few walls and broken shingles to stop one of the Pacupsy boys.

Less than ten feet separated me from that gaping wound in the side of our house. Dark as night on the inside, nothing moved other than pieces of roof and wall waiting to fall as more oil slicked every edge and floor.

I think that is where I made my first mistake. It's kind of hard to remember with the pain making everything fuzzy, ya know. But somehow the thing caught me.

Well, I'm guessing that is what happened. All the air sucked right out of my body in the blink of an eye as the world spun around. At first, I was just about an arm's length away from that front door, the handle stretching out to touch my fingers, and then the sky was taking me in a warm embrace before spitting me back out and the ground looked me square in the eye.

Never did like the idea of falling. That's why I'm not much for flying in one of those airplanes, and the ground was not too gentle as I landed back toward where our daddy's old truck waited. Mud and oil, and all kinds of nasty tastes splashed in my face as I tried to catch my breath again. Pretty sure the beast cracked a few of my ribs as it felt like knives ripping across my chest every time I breathed.

By that time, I had given up. There was no place to go. For God's sake the devil was at least fifty feet tall now, it's muscles I swear growing with each swing of its arms and legs. Looking down, I want to say it regarded me with what I would hope was sympathy as it considered what to do with my insignificant life.

Sliding across the filth was all I had left. I reached the truck and pulled myself up into a seated position. If I was going to die, I'd at least be sitting up and defying the odds without shedding a single tear.

Heat washed over me as it howled into the night. Large hands with claws as long as I am tall flexed as the monster took its damn time reaching out to rip the life from me. I could see the flicker of light on the razor edges as the black talons drew closer. I wanted to curse the thing back into the depths from which it had come. Let it take the last of my breath, but I would die knowing that in the end, my final stand would be worth writing on a tombstone of memory.

"Hey you ugly asshole!" Tobias screamed, and I let out a sigh of relief.

Pain racked my body as I turned toward the direction of the house. I had to wipe away warm oil running from the edges of my eyes to see clearly, but it was hard mistaking what I saw even between the gigantic legs of the devil himself.

There, in front of the house, black rain and mud caking his body, was my brother. A piece of wood, that looked suspiciously like a leg from my mother's dining room table, held high over his head. Flames licked hungrily at the night sky. Oil raining from one end of the yard and the hatred that radiated from Tobias' eyes was electrifying though still not enough to get me to move.

"Why don't you pick on someone your own size," Tobias challenged.

He waved the burning stick like a sword and the creature answered with a roar that shook the ground beneath me. My brother did not waver. Brandishing the piece of mother's table like a shield he waited patiently for the thing to turn fully away from me.

Backing slowly away, Tobias never wavered as the devil approached. Legs spread, shoulders held high, for once in my life I was proud of the man though I knew it would only last for the few moments it took the thing to squash him like a bug.

"In the name of God, I send you back into the depths of hell from where you came from!" Tobias commanded.

I never knew him to be much of a pious man, but in that moment, he spoke like a man of the cloth. Even better than the fat old men on Sundays who have far more practice than him.

Not to be deterred, the beast lifted one deadly arm and took a swipe at Tobias that would have cleaved him in half if it was not for our house. Shingles and siding splintered into the air and my brother rolled out of the way, the burning brand held safely above the ground.

Dodging with an agility I never knew he had, he shouted more challenges as the two combatants moved closer to the geyser of oil. I tried several times to lift myself from my predicament, but the injuries and pain were too great. I was limited to being a spectator in the fight to save the world. For surely if we did not put this monster down, here this evening, who is to know what kind of devastation it would have rot upon our world.

Rolling and scattering insults, Tobias finally stopped when they were right beside the fountain of liquid gold as it erupted from the earth. Darkness covered him from head to toe and if it wasn't for his size, I would have had a hard time distinguishing him from the monster trying to kill us. His long hair stuck to his head and face like one of those action movie stars fighting their last battle.

"Your reign of terror ends here, demon," Tobias shouted.

Raising to an even greater height, I swear the monster was now at least sixty feet tall. It made us look like ants beneath its girth as it lifted a leg to stomp my brother into the ground.

Defiantly and without hesitation Tobias struck out with his burning brand, not at the monster itself, but at the stream of oil.

Flames erupted and rose like a curtain, bright and hot all the way up until it blanketed the beast. Howls like I've never heard echoed into the night as the demon recoiled from the fire, but it was too late.

Tobias ran my way as the thing thrashed and tumbled over our house. Crashing through what remained standing, the wreckage caught on fire as dark smoke rolled from the flames as oil and demon flesh was consumed.

The stench was like nothing you could imagine. Burned demon and oil will choke the life right out of you. I could barely breathe as Tobias helped me up from the ground. I noticed a cut deep across his forehead as we climbed into the truck.

We could still see the fires over ten miles away as

we drove down the highway. Like a pile of burning tires, the fumes chased us, and we felt bad for the firefighters as they rushed to put out the flames. I thought about stopping them and telling them to let the thing burn, but I doubted they would listen. It's in their blood. Like digging for oil was in my grand-pappy's blood all the way down to us, it is just something you can't give up.

But I'm living proof right here. People change. The sins of our forefathers do not scar the lives of grand-children who look to make their own path in this world.

"Ain't that right, Tobias?"

"Huh?" he answered.

"Ah nothing, go back to working on those seals. These old sarcophagi don't open themselves you know."

The End

Goodbye Daddy

By
William J. Seymour
© 2015

Omaha was just another stop. A city of darkness and lost souls in a world consumed by madness. It was supposed to be an easy night. Get some rest, find some food, and continue on down Old Interstate 80. There wasn't supposed to be a little boy. The ghosts had said there would be another. Damn, they are always right.

"What makes a Hero?"

Merchant felt a bit of remorse for the kid, his dirty brown hair knotted from days of neglect, as he stood near the edge of the table. Such a simple question, wasn't it? One thing was for certain, sitting at a table like this, with its obscenities and the remarkably well-drawn picture of a woman's breasts carved into the wood, Heroes would be the last thing you would find here.

Against most standards, the bar was like any other dive place he had seen since he started his trek west. A smoky room filled with men either too drunk from just trying to stay alive, or too high to realize their death had already come and gone. Women, if you could still recognize them as that, scooted from table to table. They searched like scavengers for another warm bed to rest their makeup caked head, and if they were lucky, another heavy pocket to empty before the morning light brought back the reality of this dead world.

"Are you a hero, mista?" the small boy, dirt smudged on both of his white cheeks, asked as he nervously pawed over a little brown stuffed rabbit he held within his hands.

Merchant eyed the boy and the small toy. They could both use a bath. With a fresh bowl of hot water, he imagined the rabbit would be just as white as the child, but at the moment, neither of them smelled any better than they looked.

"Heroes are only bad people, kid. They are the types unlucky enough to find themselves in the wrong place, at the wrong time. You aren't going to find any heroes around here." Merchant picked up his foggy mug of what the bartender called "Omaha's strongest cider" and swallowed what remained inside.

A small fire burned in his belly as the piss warm liquid made its way down. Strong wasn't the word he would use to describe it, more like weak with a side of sour, but it was the best his coin was going to afford. Putting his stained mug back down on the wobbly table, the child remained where he stood, eyes down, bunny held tightly before him.

"Is there something else you want, kid?"

Merchant didn't normally have time for lost children, or anyone else unless the coin was right, but for some reason, this one was persistent.

"I'm looking for my parents, mista."

The little boy's eyes were a magnificent hazel with a mix of bloodshot as he refused to shy away from Merchant's gaze.

"And what makes you believe I can help you out?"

Sitting back in his rickety old bar chair, Merchant searched the room as he waited for the kid's answer. His gut was telling him he wasn't going to like what he heard. Maybe the ghosts had been right, he should have kept moving down old Interstate 80 instead of stopping, but it had been a long time since he had somewhere to sleep and something to drink. Facing those piercing little eyes, just maybe the ghosts had been right.

"I heard you had something for sale and was wondering if we could make a deal, mista."

Damn, the ghosts were always right.

* * *

The night was beginning to fill the sky as Merchant paid for the last of his drinks before grabbing his lone bag to head out the door. He hadn't been in town more than three hours and the gnawing feeling that shit was going to go from bad to worse ached in the pit of his stomach. He had grown used to this feeling, and it had taught him many times over the years not to ignore it. Shaking off the last-ditch efforts of a woman who favored herself 'Wanda the Magnificent', he threw the last good arm strap of his bag over his shoulder and exited into the night.

Stale air filled the streets as fog began to lift itself off the ground like ghosts risen to feed on what remained of the living. Looking up at the sign above the door, "BAR" was the only remnants of what was likely once a fine establishment. Listening to the laughter of drunken men and desperate women echo into the night, the singular name fit such a desperate place in desperate times.

"Walking alone at night isn't such a good idea in this part of town," a man's deep voice called from the alley ahead.

Merchant hadn't made it more than a hundred paces down the street from the entrance to the bar. This wasn't a good start. Stepping out, three men, all with clean shaven heads spread to block the path before him. The front one was a burly fellow, large around the shoulders, yet larger around the belly. Next to him, two young men flanked his sides. Both looked lucky enough to be of drinking age if that law was even still around.

"Now, what is a traveler like you, doing in a place like this?"

A small hook formed on the man's thin lips as he bounced the end of a wooden Louisville Slugger in his hands.

Two more men circled around the back. Merchant watched their shadows by the streetlamp above. A trap. Why were the ghosts always right? Merchant gripped the strap of his bag tighter, but remained silent.

"Did you hear me, boy?" Burly mocked as the others chuckled, but even five to one, his friends would not say a word of their own. "We got word that you might be in town to cause some trouble. You see me and my boys here, we don't like problems here in our part of town. Are you here to start something, huh, boy?"

Insults and bantering like this, Merchant had seen many times before. It never ended well, not for anyone involved, especially the one who brings the bat.

"I think we have a dumb one on our hands, Boss. Maybe if we string him up by his neck, we'll loosen that tongue of his," a voice snickered from the back.

Merchant couldn't see him, but the nasal voice, and nervous movements of his shadow reminded him of a weasel.

"You have thirty seconds to answer me, boy, or maybe we'll have us a little fun. It's been a long time since we had a reason to show these people why stepping out of line isn't good for anyone."

Removing his bag from his shoulder, Merchant never let his eyes leave the burly leader's face. Thick callused hands white knuckled the wooden weapon he held, his eyes refused to meet Merchant's as he moved from face to face, and his teeth bit hard enough into his lower lip to draw blood.

"Enough of this, get him, boys!" Burly ordered as Merchant ducked under the wild haymaker thrown by Weasel.

Pivoting on one foot, Merchant tried to put his back to open space and keep all five of the men in front of him. Weasel's wingman charged forward; bat cocked back and ready to swing for the game-winning home run. Dropping his shoulder, Merchant drove his body into the man's leading arm, knocking him off balance and forcing him to stagger as he caught his feet. Once balanced, the man reared back and swung with everything he had at Merchant's head. Ducking under the strike, the familiar sound of bone cracking like a ripe melon echoed in the streets as Weasel hit the ground with a thud.

"Stevie!" the man yelled in shock as he dropped his bat, his face going ghostly white at the sight of what he had just done.

"What are you two doing? Get him!" Burly commanded, stepping back while pointing his bat toward the fight.

Turning, Merchant kicked the sobbing man over the lifeless body of Stevie, rolling him into the two men who ran forward. Unable to stop, the first man never got a chance to get out of the way as his knee got caught in his tumbling partner's legs, dropping him to the ground. Jumping over his two fallen comrades, the second young man found himself in Merchant's extended arms, spinning around to strike the dusty brick wall that lined the nearest building with his face. Blood and tissue streaked down the coarse stone as his body slid down slowly, before rolling backward and thumping on the pavement.

"You motherfucker! You'll pay for this!"

Burly had a revolver out and pointed right at Merchant's head. Too much distance separated him and the gun. Guess this was the end of the road. Fucking ghosts had been right.

The hook of a smile formed again on the man's face as he pulled back the hammer on the weapon. Silence filled the air as time seemed to slow. Killing a man was easy when the odds favored you. If you were angry enough, it wouldn't take much thought. Harder still, to see your friend standing up from the ground when you allow yourself to forget everything but you and your target.

Red mist and gray smoke exploded into the street as Burly fired his revolver. Whoever the kid had been, he was nothing more than a corpse now as the back of his brain exploded when the bullet erupted within his head. Wasting no time, Merchant leaped over the bodies lying on the street, covering the distance between him and Burly before the man could consider what he had done. Slamming his fist into Burley's stomach, he shoved the fat man against the nearest wall.

"Who the fuck are you, and who told you I was in town?" Merchant growled, pressing the sharp tip of his knife against the pallid skin that covered the man's carotid artery.

"Fuck you, boy! I won't tell you nothin!"

Merchant expected as much; he let the tip of the knife draw a drop of blood.

Hissing in his ear, "I'll give you one last try. Who the fuck told you I was coming?" Each word dripped with drops of promised death. "You had better be quick about it, BOY. Fights like this always get me a little bit, excited. Against my better judgment, I may let you live."

Merchant watched as the man's Adam's apple bobbed in his throat. He could smell the fear pouring off Burly's body. Sweat ran freely down the man's forehead as he hesitated, wetting his dry lips with his tongue. His mouth moved, but the words would not come. Was he afraid of the man who set him up more than he was of dying right here in the street? Stupid men always did stupid things. Merchant pressed the knife harder as those still alive began to groan, trying to pick themselves up off the ground.

"Look, me and the boys here don't want any more trouble. Shit, Ralphie there, oh shit man, it was his birthday yesterday."

Weakness drained the strength from Burly's knees, and Merchant was forced to try to keep him standing by pressing harder on the man's chest. He didn't want the man cutting his neck before he had time to give what little information he had.

Coaxingly, Merchant said real slow, "Think man. The kid is dead, but the rest of you can live if you do something, right now. I don't know who you are, and if we end this quietly, I may leave this place without ever knowing anything more about you. Now tell me, who the fuck sent you?"

"Ah, fuck man. It was one of Snake Eye's men. Last night up at the Pleasure Palace, told us there was going to be a stranger coming through town. Said you would stick out like a sore thumb, paid us up front too." Burly swallowed hard as his eyes didn't leave the corpse on the ground. "Shit, Ralphie even got a free night with one of the top girls. Pretty Mindy as he called her. I even think it was his first time."

Merchant pulled the knife from the man's throat. He could see the tears welling up in Burly's eyes as he slumped to the ground. They would be no more trouble for him tonight, or any other night. Looking down the street, he could see the commotion had barely brought anyone out from the shadows. Gunfire and shouts didn't elicit much attention these days.

"Get the fuck out of here. Don't let me see you before I leave town. Next time, I'll think better of just giving you a scratch on the neck."

Tracing an outline on his throat, he watched as Burly struggled to get the rest of his men off the ground. Picking his bag up, Merchant looked into the foggy streets. West headed back out to old Interstate 80 and onto the next leg of his trip. East would be nothing but another headache and more death. Adjusting his bag across his back, he listened as he recognized the distinct sound of its contents. With a heavy sigh, the dark man turned east and began the long walk into the unforgiving night.

* * *

The Pleasure Palace stood out in the haze like a beacon of hope with its lights shining a path for the lost souls that wandered helplessly through this world. Outside, the palace was a modernly built office building, rectangular and fake brick reaching four stories into the air. Countless windows allowed light to stream out into the night. The shaded gyrations of the bodies were visible from the ground below.

Merchant slowed as he approached the door. Closing his eyes and focusing on the muffled sounds. An old rock band playing a song that was popular maybe twenty years ago. The rhythm of the music could be felt through the ground at his feet just as much as the sound pounded in his ears. Laughter, screams of pleasure and fear, played with the music. Shifting the bag over his shoulder one more time, Merchant grabbed the cool metal handle of the wood double doors and let himself in.

Inside, the house of the man they called 'Snake Eyes' was just as hazy as the fog filled city streets. Merchant wrinkled his nose and held back a cough as the sweet smell of marijuana rolled through the lobby like a wave crashing against a storm wall. Some patrons and workers milled around the edges of the open area, while others, barely attired, congregated in the middle playing with all that they desired. Gripping the strap to his bag tighter, Merchant shrugged and stepped forward. Spending your last days in this world wrapped in the arms of someone was not the worst thing they could do. Everyone runs from their fears in one way or another.

"So, what has caught your eye tonight, stranger?" a young girl questioned with a devilish smile from behind the receptionist's desk.

Regarding her for a moment, he could see the tight leathers she wore on her body. Strips of black found their way to cover what little the girl didn't reveal to the open world, even the white scars across her back and left cheek hung out for all to see.

"I'm just looking for a room, maybe even some-one who wouldn't mind spending a few moments talking with a fellow." Merchant turned his attention to the girls displayed around the room. He sensed that he wasn't going to get much out of them. He turned his attention back to the receptionist with a smile. "It's pretty lonely out on the road, especially when you only have ghosts and infected to talk with."

"Conversation is only a small bit of what my girls and boys are good at," a woman's voice answered from behind him with an air of pride behind it.

Merchant watched as the girl behind the counter slid away, her eyes glued to the ground at her feet as he listened to the sounds of heels clicking until they stopped a few feet behind him.

"For the right price, you can find out anything and everything you want. That is, of course, if you can afford any time at all."

The woman's voice tickled the back of his ear.

Turning around, Merchant felt the bottom of his throat roll up as his breath caught in his lungs. Standing in front of him was a sight that made him for a second lose thought of where he was. She was statuesque, and her skin a flawless porcelain. Deep blue eyes, soft high cheekbones, and a set of full lips looked him up and down as she sized him up.

Unlike all the other men and women in the room, she did not wear clothing that marked her as a working girl. Instead, she wore a full-length, dark-green evening gown. Emerald scales lined the entirety of the outfit, brilliantly reflecting the light that lit the room from a dozen angles. Eyeing her up and down himself, Merchant could feel himself stop as he found the one thing that brought him back to the reality of the smoky room. On her long white neck, was the tattoo of a coiled snake, its fangs bit into holes that dripped scarlet red blood from both sides of her throat.

"I will have enough to pay. One night is all that I will need. I don't plan on staying in town too long."

No longer transfixed by the vixen standing in front of him, Merchant noticed the young girl who coiled behind her. She was more than a head shorter and dressed like any other working girl in tight leathers revealing too much of her frail body. Her eyes didn't leave the ground except to try to steal a look at him, which she immediately stopped the moment she noticed that he saw her.

"Then I wish you a good evening, my dark stallion. Any of these girls, or boys, will bring you a night worth remembering."

With the slightest of smiles, the tall vixen turned to leave.

"What about her?" Merchant put his foot forward to stop the smaller girl from following.

"I'm not ready, sir," she said with a soft trembling voice.

Her face snapped to the side as a lightning-fast hand slapped across her face.

"Don't you start lying to men like that!" The vixen towered over the girl as she cowered on crouched knees. She turned with a smirk to Merchant. "Of course, I would personally recommend someone, of a more sophisticated taste for a man such as yourself."

Merchant could feel his hands begin to stiffen as he watched the small girl cower on her knees. Just a small drop of blood pooled at the edge of her thin lips, her cheek already turning a nasty claret red.

"No, I think I will like this one for the night."

The young worker's eyes opened wide with fear as Merchant slammed a fist full of gold coins down on the counter. With a vice-like grip, the vixen pulled the girl from her crouch and led her to stand at his side.

"As you wish." She nodded to the young woman behind the counter. "I do believe that will be more than enough for a good night's rest. We shall see you in the morning."

Taking the key left where his money had been, Merchant followed the young girl to the second floor. She didn't talk, nor did she look back at him as her shoulders remained slumped, and her shaking hands jingled the key on its chain.

Stopping at the room nearest the end of the hall, Merchant watched as she struggled to unlock the door. The tip of the key never finding the correct position as the shaking now carried down her arm and into her shoulders. Reaching out, he placed his large hand over hers and the door handle itself.

"Please, let me help. Do not fear me. I am not here for you."

With a twist of his wrist, the door opened to the shadowed room beyond. Stepping in, Merchant searched for anything within the shadows as he found the light switch on the wall. With a flick, the bright-yellow light flashed before his eyes just as lightning streaked across his vision, and his world fell silent.

***

"Is this him, Boss?" a strange male voice asked from the darkness behind him.

Ringing filled his ears, and the taste of blood filled his mouth. Searching with the tip of his tongue, he was sure at least one tooth was loose, but luckily, they were all still there. Mom always said he had a strong jaw.

"Does he look like the man you've heard stories about?" another male voice spoke, this time from in front.

Merchant kept his eyes closed and controlled his breathing. The longer he let them believe he was still out, the better chance he had of figuring out where he was and what they wanted. The slightest flex of the muscles in his arms told him all he really needed to know.

He was tied to a chair, hands bound at the wrist behind him. At least they did him the service of leaving his feet free.

"I'm tired of waiting. Wake his ass up." the second voice commanded as Merchant felt someone grab the back of his head.

Cold water splashed onto his face. The light in the room burned into his eyes as he coughed out the water from his lungs.

"Glad to see you back in the world of the living."

Merchant eyed the man as he seated himself comfortably on top of a polished wooden desk. The man dressed as ornately as he could. Bright red silk pants and shirt, six gold necklaces around his neck, and more rings than could be counted lined his fingers. Only the tattoo on his neck stuck out to Merchant. Yellow and slanted, a pair of eyes adorned each side of his throat. Snake eyes.

"You can still speak, can't you? My man here didn't knock out all your teeth, I know, I had him check," Snake-Eyes chuckled as he leaned backward.

Reaching back onto his desk, the man pulled out a rolled cigarette and lit it. The sweet smell that filled every room of the building quickly spread from the small flame. Merchant didn't respond. Silence always killed men like him.

"Gonna be the tough guy, are we?"

Snake-Eyes nodded to his assistant.

Pain and air rushed out of Merchant's lungs as the man behind him stepped up and slammed his meaty fist into his stomach. Air struggled to find its way in as his abdomen cramped with coughing.

"Did that straighten anything up?

The man lounged back as he took another drag on his cigarette. Merchant, his breath returned, spit a wad of blood down on the floor, the pain continuing to grow behind his head.

"Fuck, you are a stubborn bastard, aren't you? Well, let me tell you what I've heard." Snake eyes stood and towered over Merchant. "I've got this tiny little rumor going around my town that there is this man, what do they call him, Hank?"

"The Black Devil."

"Ah, yes, the Black Devil. They say he's making his way west on old Interstate 80. Every city he stops at, people start dying. They say if you have the money, or the 'soul' to sell, anyone you want to die will be dead before he leaves. Now, here you are. Black man, traveling west on Interstate 80, and I have to ask myself, why are you here?" Snake Eyes bent real close and blew a large puff of the sweet smoke into Merchant's face. "Well, why are you here, boy? Who are you here to kill? Who paid you to get off the highway and find your way into my city?"

Merchant didn't respond. He met the man eye-to-eye, but wouldn't respond. No answer he could give would make this go any easier. Dead men always made it harder than it needed to be.

"Gonna remain the silent type, are we?" Snake Eyes nodded and pain shot through the back of Merchant's head as it snapped forward from the blow delivered by the man standing behind him. "See, I'm almost starting to believe we have the wrong man here, Hank. Look what we found in this little bag of yours."

Merchant pulled on the bonds that held him to his chair. Thick rope scratched at his skin as his hands and forearms were tied tightly by someone who knew something about knots. With a flex of his toes and ankle, he warmed up the muscles in his lower legs.

Amateurs.

"Ah, yes. We can't do without something like this Hank, a little silver locket." Snake Eyes opened it up. "Shit, two little kids in it. They don't even look like you, my silent friend. What else do we have in here? Oh, yes, a personal journal with, 'I love Travis' circled in a heart on it."

One of Snake-Eyes' eyebrows lifted as he looked at Merchant. He returned to the journal and flipped through a few pages. Dropping the book to the floor, frustration began to show on the man's face as he went through the bag piece by piece. Merchant watched as he discarded each item until something in the bag had him stop and stand in silence for just a moment.

"Junk. You have nothing but random pieces of junk in this tired old bag of yours."

Snake-Eyes walked up and stood hovering over Merchant, the strong smell of stale alcohol and weed radiated off the man.

"What is this, a bunny rabbit?"

The man held a dirty little toy in his hands as he dropped the bag and the rest of its contents to the floor.

"You know, I used to have a kid. Did you know that, Hank?"

Merchant watched as the man pawed the soft, dirty toy.

"No, I didn't boss."

"You wouldn't. He was a weak little thing. Didn't take much for me to convince our sweet Madame to leave the little bastard behind. He didn't have what a real man needs in this world. Always crying, wanting food and attention. Little shit needed to learn you take what you want in this world. You can't just wait until someone gives it to you. We've been better off since we rid ourselves of that burden." Snake-Eyes bent close until his nose was almost touching Merchant's. "Now my question again. Why do you have a little toy bunny rabbit, like the one that weak little kid of mine used to have? Tried to make a man out of him yourself, did you?"

Snake-Eyes sneered as he looked up to Hank for confirmation of the joke. Merchant took a deep breath as he steadied himself.

"Payment."

Bloodshot eyes opened wide as the realization hit the man the same moment Merchant's forehead smashed into his nose. Blood squirted out as Snake-Eyes reeled back. Kicking out with his free foot, Merchant's boot connected with the side of the man's knee with a familiar sound of bone and ligaments snapping.

"Ah!"

Merchant leaned forward and picked up the chair that held itself tightly against him. With a grunt, he charged backward, legs of the chair tilted high as he pumped what he could with his legs. Creaky wood and nails met flesh and bone as he crashed into Hank, still too slow to react.

Both men crashed to the ground as the chair that held Merchant shattered to pieces. No longer restrained by the wooden frame, the ropes that bound him tight slipped to the ground. Merchant rolled over and slammed his fist into Hank's face. The man grunted as he tried to cover his head. Another blow sent the man's eyes rolling back into his head.

"You fucking bastard. I'm going to string you up for this!"

Merchant heard the words followed by the familiar click of a hammer locking back from across the room. Not taking the time to look, he pushed with his legs as he rolled forward. Two rounds exploded into Hank's chest, right where Merchant had been only a split second before.

Puffs of fiber floated in the air as more rounds tore through the couch Merchant rolled behind. He kept moving as Snake-Eyes continued to fire. Bullet after bullet exited the back of the furniture, mere inches from his body.

The end of the leather sofa neared as pain seared through his body as Snake Eye's next shot exited the back and sank deep into Merchant's left arm.

"Hurts doesn't it? You fucking bastard!"

Empty metal dropped to the floor as the man went to reload his weapon. Using the large desk for support, he struggled to get the next magazine in so he could put a round into the chamber as his blood-covered hands slipped on the metal casings.

Without a word, Merchant, using his good arm, flipped the nightstand at the end of the couch. The oil lamp that burned on the piece crashed to the ground, shattering and spreading the burning oil around Snake-Eye's feet.

"What the fuck!"

Snake-Eyes gave up trying to reload his weapon as he kicked at the flames. The oil spread quickly. The man's meager attempts only helped spread the fire.

Merchant, seizing the opportunity, jumped from behind the couch, a leg of the broken chair lifted high over his head. He let it crash down on Snake-Eyes' right hand, shattering the tiny bones within and sending the gun skidding across the ground.

"Fuck!"

Grabbing his destroyed hand, Snake-Eyes barely got a glance as Merchant next swing met with the side of his chin. Blood sprayed out as several teeth clattered to the floor. The blood and flesh still attached sizzled in the flames.

"What are you going to do?" Snake-Eyes muttered.

Backing away, the man tried to keep his hand between him and Merchant, but only succeeded in bringing it back to his mangled face.

Merchant moved slowly forward. Flames behind his back, he led the man toward the window that overlooked the street below.

"I have money. I have girls." The words slurred, and blood poured out as Snake Eyes tried to bargain.

"Take whatever you want. Just get us out of here. his whole place is going to burn."

They were directly in front of the window now. Looking over Snake Eyes' shoulder, Merchant could see their shadows on the street below. The light from the flames flickered behind their dark images.

"I don't want anything from you." Snake Eye's eyes widened as Merchant reached for the small rabbit that had fallen next to the wooden desk. "There is a message I am supposed to give you, though."

Tears ran from the man's eyes as he tried to hold his jaw in place. Merchant could see the pain on the man's face, his cheek now swollen and going black.

"From a little boy I met in town." Merchant took a deep breath before smiling. "Good-bye, Daddy."

Glass erupted into the night air as a man's body propelled its way into the unforgiving space between the ground and the window. Everyone outside on the street, still struggling to make their way into the Palace itself, filled the night with their screams. Blood and what remained of the man's body slowly spread its way down the pavement, mixing with the dirt and grime that covered the road.

* * *

Dark smoke rose high into the air, its column silhouetted by the flames that lit the sky like a new day's rising sun. Merchant could hear the screams of people both running away from the blaze, and those making their way closer, moving secretly in the hope of finding a way to profit from this night's strange events.

The road he followed headed west, and there was still a lot of ground to cover before he finally made it to the land where the road met the sky. Old Interstate 80 was his guide, and it laid waiting outside the city. Merchant knew he'd be out in the open soon, once again alone. Nothing but him, the infected, and the ghosts.

He'd keep moving. He was promised no rest until his journey was done. Walking through Omaha's deserted streets, his surroundings began to grow familiar. A small feeling grew like butterflies in his stomach at the sight of the single word "Bar" that told him that once again he had fulfilled his sale.

The door to the old dive was open. Some patrons had passed by, curiosity bringing them outside against all their fears of what the night held, but they would soon return. This part of town, people stayed away from anything that they didn't know. Familiarity made them feel safer. Strange and unexpected things brought danger and death. Merchant could feel their fear, it permeated this world, and it remained here like every other city along the old interstate.

Standing in the doorway, the small light from within the building stretched the shadows of two figures he recognized. The little boy, his piercing hazel eyes stared out at him, and the wrinkled hand of Wanda's rested comfortably on his shoulder. In his small hands, the boy no longer held that small dirty rabbit, nor was his attention held by the ground at his feet. Even from across the street, Merchant could see the upturned lips, and the distinct fire that burned behind the child's eyes.

Twirling and dancing between the little man's fingers was the razor-sharp edge of a well-maintained carving knife. Merchant chuckled to himself as the kid allowed the knife to disappear and reappear in his hands with practiced ease. A small nod and silent acknowledgment are all that passed between them as Merchant continued up the road. Adjusting the weight of the pack that he carried on his back, he could feel the small rabbit that shifted and settled with everything else inside.

He knew every last item that filled the burden he carried. Three years now, each city he passed brought him something else that weighed him down as he continued to travel west. His life was his curse. His path to walk. If the ghosts that followed him were right, he'd have a collection only a monster could carry before he was done. He wasn't a monster. Just a single man, a lonely merchant in a world lost to oblivion. But, if the price was right, every life was for sale, and there was no greater salesman than the one they called, Merchant.

The End

Angel on the Edge

By
William J. Seymour
© 2015

Humanity lost its struggle against the Demons and their minions decades ago. Now all that remains are the final holdouts of civilization, untouched and hidden from the evil that has destroyed the world. Dale believes she is out there protecting them. To everyone else she is a myth, a fairytale to help young children sleep at night. Dale knows better, for he has seen her, and she needs his help.

"Do you think she even notices us?" Dale asked while he scratched at the dry dirt with his handheld cultivator.

The earth was bone dry. There hadn't been any rain in over a month and the crops that still clung to life were showing signs that this may be the end.

"Why would she?" Kevin answered as he wiped the sweat from his brow. Replacing his Redskin ball cap with the ripped visor and sun-bleached emblem, Dale could see the dirt that smeared over his best friend's red cheeks.

Mid-day had passed several hours ago, yet the temperature continued to rise. A dry wind whistled across the land carrying with it sand that scratched at their throats as the two boys worked tirelessly in the community garden.

"She has to notice someone. Why else would she protect us from the darkness?" Dale continued as he grabbed a thin stem of thistle and tore it from the ground.

Vegetables and fruits struggled to germinate in the dry, arid land, yet weeds grew no matter how much they worked the beds.

"You believe that old wives' tale, don't you?" Kevin chuckled as he leaned against the long handle of his rake. "She's an angel protecting us from the demons that have destroyed this world. One of the last warrior's sent to save us from the madness that has consumed us all."

Dale looked up at his friend, the bright sun burning the light blue sky behind him. Kevin was half a foot taller and carried himself like his father. Wide at the shoulders, though their food was scarce, the men of his family still filled out their stalky frames. He on the other hand never knew his father, but it didn't matter. Everyone said he took after his mother's side. Pale skin that was prone to burning, his freckles extended from the patch of red hair that grew over his ears to the ends of his fingers. Watching the muscles of his forearm move as he squeezed his hand, he shook his head. Too skinny and too hungry.

"Oh my, you do believe them, don't you?" Kevin chuckled as kicked his heels together dancing behind his rake.

"Shut-up!" Dale threw a handful of dry dirt at his friend before turning back to the row of radishes struggling to survive. "You've heard the stories just as much as I have. They can't all be lies."

He could feel the embarrassment swell up behind his cheeks, which he knew were already burned red from the sun.

"No, but you still amaze me my friend." Kevin knelt down beside him to reach and pull out a handful of thistles himself. "The world fell apart decades ago, and we all know why. Terrorists and wars. Not those children's stories that old grandma Shirley used to tell us. There are no such things as demons and angels fighting to save us from or doom us to damnation."

Kevin stood up, his hands on his hips as he stretched his back. Sweat stains marked the underarms and chest of his white tee-shirt though Dale felt as if his shirt was soaked.

"You never know. She's out there. We all know it," Dale whispered to himself, wincing as a sharp needle of thistle bit into his skin.

"What I do know is there are rumors of a crazy woman who survives in the Whispering Woods," Kevin said while leaning forward on his rake. "I haven't seen her, but my father says she's as rabid as the starving dogs that hunt at night. She isn't some angel, let alone our savior. You're my friend Dale, but you need to grow up."

Dale squinted as he looked up with anger and sadness churning within him.

"Plus, your gardening needs work. Those radishes look half dead, and I heard that the harvest this year is going to be our worst yet," Kevin said as he leaned his rake against the rusted chicken wire fence that marked the boundary of the garden. "Even an angel won't be able to save us if we all starve to death."

With a pat on Dale's shoulder, Kevin chuckled one more time before walking toward the dusty homes that clustered together in the center of the village.

Dale sighed to himself as he watched for signs of movement within the ghostly confines of the Whispering Woods. White sun-bleached husks stretched high into the air, the branches brittle and gnarled as they warped from the sun's relentless heat. She was out there, somewhere in the shadows, and she protected them all. It wasn't just a children's story because he had seen her. In his dreams, she was there, guarding against the evil that threatened them all. Deep within him, he knew the truth. One day, he'd prove it to them all and himself. He would find the angel at the edge of their darkness.

* * *

She walks toward him. Long legs and soft brunette hair flows behind her as if blessed by the word of God himself. Light shines down from above; the darkness pushed back as she floats through the brush of the hollow trees toward him. He can no longer move his arms or legs as he is helpless in her presence. Her face carries with it a smile, one that melts his heart as her ruby red lips curl ever so slightly upward toward her dark eyes.

She is an angel, and he knows it to be true. There is no question in his heart, the darkness itself cannot approach her. As she nears him, he can feel his muscles tense. There is power here, and it radiates from her and presses against him like a warm blanket. The evil that permeates the land can no longer harm him. She is here to protect them all. She walks this earth to protect God's remaining children. It is her mission; it is her charge.

Warmth fills his chest as she is almost upon him. Only a few rotten oak trees, brightened by the approach of God's champion stands between them. He can feel the sweat running down his forehead. He tries to wipe it away, but his arms are of no use as he struggles to breathe. She knows who he is, and he knows she is real. The others do not understand, they do not believe. But they also do not love her like he does.

His knees grow weak, and he could not rise to his feet if he tried. She is almost to him as he can feel the smile that stretches across his face. Yes, he loves her, and he knows what she does for them. He will make the others believe; he will show them, and in the end, he will be one with her.

Her feet stop a step before him. Pain burns in his eyes as the light above shines and blocks the beauty of her face. Her skin is pale enough to be a ghost, her silk dress so thin he can see every curve of her body as the cloth hugs her tightly.

"Why do you not show them?" he asks before his mouth goes dry.

There is no answer as she remains still, though he can feel a shift in the wind. A dry breeze rustles the leaves as it dances its way through the forest. He can see that her muscles have tensed though she has not moved. Shadows encroach the light that encircles them both though its power is still blinding.

"What is happening?" he chokes out before the last of his air seeps from his lungs.

She remains silent as she turns to the shadows that inch out from behind the graves of Mother Nature's beauty. Light erupts from her beautiful hand as a blade appears as if by magic. He tries to breathe, but he can't, his eyes lost to the magnificence of the weapon she holds. Light and power flows through the blade, a promise of righteousness and forgiveness that carries down its sharpened edge.

He can feel the darkness clouding his vision. His eyes struggle to remain open as he watches her step toward the approaching darkness. He tries to call to her, but there is nothing to say. In vain he can only reach out his shaking hand. His love, and his angel, is leaving him.

"Find me," her voice carries into his mind before his world is lost to darkness.

* * *

Dale shot up in bed, his breathing erratic as his chest struggled to fill with air. Shivers ran down his back as he swallowed to fill his lungs, and the clammy feeling of sweat clung to his skin. Looking around, he could see that it was deep into the night, and he was still in his bed. Running his hands down his face, the stickiness of sweat still lingered on his palms as he felt the pulse of his heart slow.

Moonlight streamed in through the open window of his room, the thin curtains motionless in the night air. Small bits of dust filtered through the rays as he turned and placed both of his bare feet on the wood floor. The heat of the room felt stuffy as his breaths finally returned to a slower pace.

With a stiff push, he lifted himself off his straw

bed and made his way to the window. Outside their home, the night was silent and dead. The moon above moved across a sky bare of clouds, and as dark and devoid of rain as the world around him was of life. He could see the forest, a land of deceased memories stretching toward the hills to the west. Darkness filled everything that surrounded them, a blanket that they could not shake.

"Find Me"

Her words played in his mind. Soft and magical, the voice was a song that could play forever, and he would never tire of it. But there was something there. It was hidden out in the shadows that held them all to this small village. She needed him, and he could feel it. It wasn't a dream, nor was it a fantasy of a young man living with fairy tales he should have given up years ago. No, this was real, and he could feel it in his heart. He could sense it down to the deepest part of his soul.

She needed him; she was in trouble, and he was the only one who knew. No one else would help. With a quick turn to the worn bunk seated at the end of his bed, Dale opened the lid and cringed as the rusted hinges scratched into the night. No one made a sound in the silent house as he waited. Once he was certain he was still the only one awake, he grabbed his last remaining set of decent clothes and closed the chest as quietly as he could.

Switching from a colorless cotton shirt and pants, gritting his teeth against the heat, he put on a thicker wool shirt and the only denim pants he had left that wasn't torn up to his knees. The rough material itched at his arms as he searched his room. It was hidden, and this early in the morning he couldn't remember where he put it. Working the memories through his clouded mind, he walked himself through the last time he had seen it.

With a sigh, he sat down on the bed. It had to be somewhere here in this room. If his mother had discovered what he hid, she would have beaten him red and turned it into the village keeper. No, it was still here. He could feel it. Looking back at the window, he wished he could see his angel again. The confidence and peace he felt when she was near left him empty when he was alone, and here within the village of survivors he always felt alone.

Reluctantly, he knew he could wait no longer. He would have to venture out without it. Maybe he would get lucky and find her without being seen. The shadows were thick, and silence filled the evening air. Holding his breath, he didn't know if he would be that lucky as he slowly bent to tie his boots. She needed him, and his time was running out.

Laces tied; he lifted his head from down at his feet to look out the window one more time. There was a large world out there, and he didn't even know where to start. For a moment he considered sneaking over to Kevin's, but he knew better. His angel was only a story to his best friend. He'd probably try to talk him out of it, and he could not afford that.

With a shake of his head, he placed his hands on his knees and went to push himself off the ground when his eye caught a small scratching under the windowsill. As quiet as a mouse, Dale made his way over. Running his fingertips under the rough wood, he could feel the small markings that cut into its surface. At the right edge, his index finger pushed through a false board and with a gasp he caught the cover before it fell to the ground. Reaching in, he felt for what he knew had to be there.

His heart skipped a beat as the one-and-a-half-foot long box slid out from behind the wall. The container was solid oak that showed no signs of wear, only a thin layer of dust that covered its smooth surface. Replacing the board beneath the window, Dale lifted the cover and bit his lower lip as the moonlight sparkled off the blade. It was a silver dagger. Over a foot long, it was a solid piece of craftsmanship without a single imperfection. The edge was as sharp as a needle and the leather hilt was oiled and without a stain.

Three years earlier, he had discovered the weapon buried in a box that his mother had hidden on her side of the house. It was a cold winter, and the village was looking for things to burn when she had sent him to find anything that would catch a flame. Rummaging through a few useless keepsakes he had found the magnificent box and the weapon it held. All around the treasure were faded photos of his mother and father though the man's face was always cut off or ruined beyond recognition.

She had always forbidden him from asking anything about the man, even others within the small community of survivors refused to talk about him. Gift in hand, he had kept his find a secret. The blade must have been from him, it was the only thing that made sense to his fifteen-year-old mind. He didn't know why his mother hated him so much, but in his heart, he knew he wanted to know more. If keeping this dagger was one step closer to having him around, Dale knew he needed it in his life.

With a push, he hid the box under his bed as he stood and slid the knife into his belt. Where he was going, he might need it, and if his mother found the box, it wouldn't matter. He was going to find the Angel in the woods and prove to everyone that she was real. She protected them, kept them safe from the horrors of this world, and tonight she needed his help. He would not let her down.

* * *

Darkness surrounded Dale as he continued down the path to the Whispering Woods. Fires lit to shield the village from the shadows of the forest burned behind him as he covered the ground between home and his angel as quickly as he could. Above, the moonlight provided a beacon of light that filled the night with a sense of peace as the soft glow encircled the small village and those that remained asleep. Two men walked the grounds throughout the night, vigilant for any beasts that roamed the countryside looking for food that was left unprotected, but they were on the opposite side.

It took a single attempt for him to escape the fencing that housed them, the sentry's occupied with following their paths more than policing the villagers. Their home had not seen nor heard anything come from the darkness of the woods for some time. Many believed it was because God had blessed them, their location still hidden from their enemies within this world. Dale knew, though; she was out there, and she kept the evil at bay.

As he approached the first set of red oaks that stretched high into the night, he could sense the difference in the air. The darkness pressed onto his skin like a film of oil as it masked all movements as he stepped further into the darkened forest. Oak trees, maples, and elms gnarled in death quickly filled in along the path. Pieces of bark crunched under his feet as sharpened twigs caught on his sleeves, pointed yet brittle as they snapped and fell to the dry earth.

With a turn back, the shadows of the forest had already blocked all vision of the village that was no more than a few dozen yards away. Closing around him, the world he had known became a land of nightmare with darkness fighting desperately to swallow him whole. The lantern extended down the path; he struggled as he pushed the fear down into his gut. He could never forget that it was there, the shiver of doubt running up his spine, but it remained a constant reminder as he continued forward.

Minutes turned to hours in his mind as he continued over fallen logs and through dried bushes. There was no clear passage, no indication of which way to go other than the pull he felt within his chest. A small voice whispered in his ear, beckoning him forward and warning him every time he strayed from the path.

His shoulders ached, and his feet felt raw as he continued along. The silence of the trees was unnerving, the air stagnant and filled with an unmistakable stench of dust. With every step he took, his nerves continued to battle his need to continue. He was lost and, in his mind, he knew he'd be lucky to find his way home before morning. If he ever found it at all. Maybe she wasn't out here. Could it all have been a dream? With his hand shaking the half-empty oil lantern, he reached down to place his hand on the hilt of his father's dagger.

He was shivering though it was too warm to be cold. Fear iced his veins as he sought anything that he could use to stabilize himself. Warm against his skin, the soft leather welcomed the touch as his hand molded around the grip, his fingers wrapping as if holding the weapon was as natural as breathing.

"You must run, go, now!" her voice broke the silence.

Pulling the blade from his belt, he held it out in front of him as his light shook and forced the shadows to dance to the beat of his frightened heart.

"Why are you here?" her voice asked, desperation laced within her words. "Stupid. You know the rules. The forest is forbidden. At night I cannot protect you."

She was near; she had to be. He could feel her magic as it pressed against him like a cloth drying in the summer breeze. There was movement in the darkness. Shadows flowed between trees as thick as smoke, waves of darkness circling him as he backed himself against the hollow shell of a forgotten maple tree.

"Do you not hear me?" her voice was frantic as the black abyss of the forest pushed closer.

Flickering, Dale watched as the tiny flame of his lantern waxed and waned. A lot of the fuel had burned, but plenty remained though the fire struggled.

"I cannot hold them. Why are you here?"

Her voice was screaming in his head. She was all around him, but so was the evil that seeped in from the woods. Deep growls circled around him. Guttural and rabid, he could sense the demons as they moved closer. His father's dagger shook as he held it out in front of him, its point reflecting the light as it moved back and forth.

Shadows were only a few steps away. Darkness had filled in all but the light that reached out no farther than his arms. Dale could feel his knees giving in. The fear inside so cold his heart pounded a rapid cadence behind his ears.

"They are here, run now!" she screamed.

Bright white light flashed before his eyes as the darkness erupted around him. Yelps and howls echoed through the forest as a path opened before him. His feet would not move as the black shadows rolled around the forest floor like a ball of dark yarn. Rays of golden light spit out as the dark mass tumbled through the brush, crushing the brittle corpses of long withered bushes and forest grass.

"Run!"

Her voice rang clear within his mind as Dale pushed away from the maple tree. Rumbling trembled the forest floor at his feet as a shadow as tall as the gnarled canopy above his head approached slowly. With feet made of lead, Dale backed his way toward the path that moved away from the struggle. He could feel the evil that permeated the air around the demon. Pillars of darkness spewed as the mass continued toward him, the light that had saved him now plunging its way further away into the shadows.

"Now!"

Dale waited no longer as he spun on his heels and ran with every ounce of adrenaline he could muster. Light splashed around him as the lantern shook violently with his retreat, the warmth of his father's blade radiating along his arm as he pushed himself harder. Branches and dry tendrils of brittle vine cut into him as he pushed forward. The rumbling of the ground grew fainter in the distance.

Sweat dripped down his face and stung his cheek as it ran over the scratches that now tore his skin. He could no longer hear her, the pounding of his heart a thunder that chased him like the shadows that were quickly closing in. Ahead he could see the path that was set for him begin to close. Held in death, the trunks of the forest twisted in an embrace as they created a wall, their limbs joined in a final dance of defiance.

Not wanting to slow, Dale pushed forward as his eyes searched for a clearing. The distance between him and the end was closing as he could feel the arms of shadows reaching out for him, grabbing at his ankles as his strength began to reach its limit. Searching, the light from his lantern showed no opening within the barrier that prevented him from leaving the shadows.

Trapped.

There was nowhere to turn as he slowed and threw himself against the wall. Nothing moved as he fell to his knees beside the barrier of hollow wood. It took what remaining strength he had to get back on his feet. He pressed his back against the end of the path. He willed his breathing to slow as he watched the darkness close in.

Slow at first, the demons took their time. Humans no longer ventured into the darkness that filled their world. Their lives and understanding long ago lost to the wars that had taken so many. Dale could feel the slow stink of death begin to climb his body. Tiny and without strength, the flame in his lantern struggled to remain lit. Burned down to nothing but a crescent orange flame, his light and his only hope was almost gone.

"Please save me, God. Where is your angel?" Dale whispered as he closed his eyes.

Sharp bark bit into the skin of his back as he pressed himself against the wood as hard as he could. He knew if he opened his eyes his world would be as devoid of light as he felt with his eyes closed. He could hear them breathing, and his skin crawled as he felt the tiny hands walk up his skin, poking and prodding to find a way inside.

"Please!" Dale shouted as the sickness washed down his spine in a tidal wave of emotion.

Shock and pain lanced through his ankles as he felt the thorny vines wrap around his legs. He could feel the fire begin to race itself up his veins as the tendrils squeezed harder, wrapping his pants in a knot at his boots.

"Ah!" Dale screamed as a bolt of electricity shot up his extremities, his thigh muscles cramping in response.

With his back against the wall, he reached down to try and grab the vines that now held him prisoner. Heat radiated from the vegetation as his hands wrapped around the moist limbs, and the spines caught on his skin. Blood tickled his fingertips as he realized his eyes were still closed. Opening them he could see through the feint light, that his palms were dripping as the thorns had ripped a gash through his hands.

"You are mine," a deep throaty voice rumbled in Dale's ears as the shock stood him back up.

Darkness had overtaken everything as his lantern was no more than a hot wick that awaited a new flame.

"Please…"

Dale's voice failed him as his bindings squeezed tighter around his ankles, the pain buckling his knees. With a yank, the young man found himself face first on the ground, his mouth full of dust and dry pine needles as he lifted his face to the darkness above. Red eyes stared back at him, their power burning with magic and hatred as the vines choked the blood from his feet and pulled him through the wall.

* * *

"A human, out here once again," her voice was soft but laced with anger. "As if my job wasn't hard enough. What could this boy have been thinking?"

Dale felt the crust on his eyes as they struggled to open. He was lying in the dirt, the hard earth a flat board as his lower back ached. A nagging itch irritated his ankles, his skin was swollen, and his muscles were sore from the cramping.

The sky above him was clear and dark with thousands of stars shining down from the distant heavens like beacon's calling a traveler home. The wind whistled a strange fairytale-like melody as it tickled the fine hairs on his arms, the air fresh and cool with a hint of moisture.

"Our boy, the adventurer, finally awakes."

Dale could hear her voice, young and strong, but full of confidence he knew he didn't have.

"I heard you pray out there, so don't go trying to tell me you don't speak," she said.

With a look around, Dale pushed himself up until he was seated, his breath stolen as he took in his surroundings. He was in a small forest alcove, walled in on all four sides by the same gnarled trees that had proven detrimental in his retreat from the demons of the darkness. Ferns and tall grass grew all along the natural barrier, swaying in the soft breeze like dancers celebrating the night. In the center of the small clearing was a pool of dark water, its surface reflecting the moonlight above as tiny waves rippled from the center.

"Where am I?" Dale asked, his voice a harsh scratch against his throat. "Am I dead?"

"You would be," she said, this time behind him. "If it wasn't for Learnie over there."

Dale spun on his seat and pushed back as his new companion came into view. She was as tall as he was with golden blond hair that laid softly over her broad shoulders. Soft high cheekbones framed her face with skin as pale as the moon above, but her eyes stopped him the moment he saw them. Softly set against her face, they were dark and depthless, an endless pool. He could feel his soul becoming lost in her vision.

"Who…Who is Learnie?" Dale asked, his heart racing as he licked his dry lips.

"Learnie would be your only friend here other than me," she said as she leaned against the encampment wall right beside him, forcing him to push himself away without knowing why. "Of course, if I weren't around, you'd probably be his lunch."

She walked over toward the water, her movements graceful, and her steps confident as she didn't look to see if he was following.

Was this the angel he had been called to find? Do all angels look like this?

With a grimace, Dale pulled himself to his feet, the itching of his ankles grew to a small burn before settling once again to an irritation he forced himself to ignore.

"Where is this Learnie, and where am I?"

"So full of questions, and yet you should be answering ours. You'd be dead like the rest if we didn't risk our necks keeping you alive."

Dale flinched at the sharp look in her eyes before her features softened, and she smiled as she dipped the tips of her fingers into the water. He didn't know what to say or think as the small oasis within the dead forest remained silent. She had to be the angel that protected them from the demons; he was certain of it, but she wasn't at all what he had imagined.

Leather straps held metal plating that fit tight against her body. Unlike knights he read about in history books and fairy tales, her outfit was tightly fit to her body though it allowed her to move with perfect grace. Reflecting the light of the moon above, he could see the metal plates that were hidden beneath the thick leather as it protected and hugged her curves.

"Come, my friend, meet who has given us such a headache," she whispered into the night air.

Rumbling echoed in the small alcove as the center of the pool began to ripple violently. The outside perimeter of the water began to swirl as the entire pond became an eddy as the shadows sank below the surface. Dale backed up a few steps while his eyes watched the head of a creature, scaly and covered in mud, slowly rise from the depths. With two heads, elongated at the nose and with forked tongues like a serpent, Dale watched as it extended itself fifteen feet above the water. Its arms were vine-like limbs that puckered with thorns from its clawed hands all the way to its shoulders. They snaked their way across the top of the dark liquid as the creature settled itself, and the spiraling water calmed as it waded into the center of the pond. The burning in Dale's ankles returned as he eyed the razors that had cut deep into him.

"He is sorry about that," she replied as if she could read his mind. "He really can't stop the poison once he wraps onto his prey. I made sure he only injected you with enough to pull you through to safety. It will go away in a few days if you are still alive."

She turned and walked back to where he had awoken. For the first time, he saw the small single bed that remained no more than five feet from where he had been laying. Vines stretched between two bare tree trunks with soft leaves the size of Dale's head laid down to build a simple looking hammock. A single chair made of a stump and curved branches sat beside it.

"What do you mean if I am still alive?"

The words stumbled as they left his lips, and

his heart began to race again as dread tickled down his spine.

"You do want to go home, don't you?" She smiled as she pushed the netting of the bed back to seat herself before lifting her feet to sway into the air. "I assume you didn't come out here to live by yourself or commit suicide. Well, I assumed that was the case."

An inquisitive look passed over her face as a silence fell between them.

"I did want to go home, but not before I found you."

"Find me?" She sat forward with her feet firmly planted on the ground and her chin resting in her cupped hands. "Now why would you want to find me, and what makes you think I would want to be found."

"You're an angel, and you protect my village."

Her laughter echoed so loudly he was sure it had reached Heaven itself. Even the large hydra churned the water behind him.

"An angel? What religious rhetoric have they got you believing in that small village you call home?" She rose to her feet and began walking away from him and around the water. Her look turned to the sky above before she continued. "You're just a dreamer kid. Playing games with his life and making mine more difficult."

"Then you're not the angel that called to me? I swore I've seen you before, in my dreams."

"Boys see many women in their dreams. Sometimes it can make them do 'silly' things with themselves when they are alone."

She continued to walk along the perimeter of the wall, and he was surprised to find himself following.

"This wasn't just a dream, I could feel it, even when I was awake."

He followed her closely though she did not turn or indicate she cared.

"OK, tell me. What did I say to you in these dreams? Was I naughty?"

She chuckled as she flicked a small pebble into the dark pool.

In response, the hydra slashed one of its arms into the water sending a jet of spray high into the air and splattering against the wooden barrier.

"No!" Dale answered in a voice meant to defend the angel from his dreams. "Most of the time you didn't say or do anything. You just watched over us. But lately things have changed."

She stopped in her tracks so suddenly he almost stumbled into her.

"How have things changed?" she asked; her head tilted so he could see the side of her face though her eyes remained looking ahead.

"Lately you have been coming to me directly, whispering that I needed to find you." He hesitated as she didn't respond, the images from his last dream vivid in his mind. "The last one you stood right in front of me until the shadows closed in. You had a weapon, a sword of light like nothing I've ever seen before."

Dale could feel his heart continue to race as she turned a little more toward him, the look on her face inquisitive, yet enough to stop him dead.

"And?" she asked impatiently.

"Oh yes, you turned back to face the darkness alone, but not without telling me I must come to find you. I needed to find you."

Silence quickly became the third wheel between them again as neither of them spoke for a few moments.

"Dreams of a young boy. This time they almost got you killed."

She waved him off as she turned and began walking once more. The ground at their feet began to dry as Dale noticed the scuff marks from something being dragged from the wall.

"Look, can you tell me the truth?" Dale pleaded. His soul was crumbling as the angel he knew existed stood right before him, yet she was still no closer. "Who are you if you aren't an angel?"

She stopped. A small sigh escaped her lips before she turned to face him. In the moonlight, her hair was almost white as it waved and fell gently across her shoulders.

"You have no need to know who or what I am. It is best we get you back to your village before anyone notices you are gone, and I'm stuck with a whole lot of you running around this forest. Keep your dreams to yourself next time kid, listen to your friends, and stay out of the forest."

With her final words, they approached the wall where most of the soil had been disturbed. From the outside, he had been unable to see any weakness in the barrier, the gnarled trees an impenetrable force. As she ran her hand across the dry bark, he could see where small fissures worked their way up along the limbs to form the entryway that the hydra must have used to drag him in.

"OK, if you are going to send me home, can you at least tell me if you saw my father's dagger?

Dale could feel the emptiness on his belt, as heavy as his heart in his stomach. He hadn't thought about it until the idea of venturing back out into the forest finally settled in his mind. Everything he dreamed of was crushed. His angel, the one woman who meant more to him than the world, didn't care for him at all. He was just another villager who needed to stay behind the wall.

"If you had it with you when you came in, it is probably still around here. Learnie has no need for the things, and I haven't seen it," she replied before she whispered a few words that Dale could barely hear.

Cracks opened, and dry bark flaked off the wall as the doorway to the forest began to take shape. Dale fought the urge to back away as he forced himself to examine the grass by his feet. He must have dropped it when he was dragged through, maybe it even caught itself in some of the vines.

Desperation began to build slowly inside as he could see her standing there watching. She didn't want to wait any longer, her right foot tapping the ground as Dale dropped to his knees.

"It's the only thing I have left from my father. I was never given the chance to know the man," Dale said while trying to hide the tremble in his voice.

Her features softened for a moment, her foot no longer tapping as she looked down at him.

"Sometimes our fathers are still around, even if you don't see them," she replied though her face looked sad. "That's at least what I tell myself."

"You lost your father as well?" Dale asked, the small sensation of relief struggled to take hold as she crouched to help.

"People would say that, but I am not so sure."

"What do you mean? How could you not know?"

"Be quiet and keep looking," she answered with a voice that would allow no argument. "I'll help you for a few more minutes, and then we are gone."

"Wait! I see something."

Dale's heart stopped for a moment as the polished metal surface of the blade caught the moonlight above when he pushed away the knee-high grass that lined the wall. The blade had sliced its way into the wood, splintering several inches into the dead tree.

"That looks," she said but hesitated with the rest.

He could feel her stand and back away as he cleared the rest of the weeds and revealed the wrapped hilt and blade.

"Are you sure that is your father's?" she asked, now standing near the dark pool with the Hydra, who was churning the water.

"Of course," he replied as he reached for the weapon.

Warmth flooded his veins the moment his skin touched the oiled leather grip, and the shadows within the hideaway retreated before him. A bright light exploded before his vision as he stumbled away from the wall, dagger in hand as the hard ground caught his fall, and the breath retreated from his lungs.

With a push from his elbows, he turned to his angel and her pet, but she was no longer there. What stood before him was the same angel from his dreams. Long golden hair fell gently over her bare shoulders as a thin dress of fine silk hugged her body as it gracefully swayed in the air until it settled at her feet.

The Hydra was no longer a two-headed serpent. Light danced and swayed as it circled an older man, naked as the day he was born decades before. Darkness and shadow orbited within the light around him, his features lost as the thunderous clouds of magic pulled at his being but retreated in an unending fight with the darkness that radiated from him like an aura.

"What… What is this?" Dale asked, lifting the blade to his face.

Untouched blue steel stretched out before him. Hammered to perfection, the knife was no longer a simple dagger, but the pristine blade of a sword with etchings of a language he could not read.

"Where did you get that?"

He could hear her voice; it was distant and had no effect as his eyes were drawn to the light that pulsed from within the power of his weapon.

"I said, where did you get that?"

Dale felt the strong hands as they gripped the front of his shirt and forcibly lifted him from the ground. He could see her face reflected in the light, but her beauty was no match for the grace of the shining white light. It warmed him down to his core, a feeling he had not known in all of his life.

"Give me that!" she shouted as she wrenched the blade from Dale's hand.

An explosion ripped the space between them as Dale tumbled into the black pool. Cool water filled his boots as he pulled himself free from the watery embrace, mud and seaweed dripping from his shirt. His angel rested against the forest barrier, the soil and bushes blown to the side where her body collided with the wall. Remaining on the ground was his father's dagger, silent and untouched, the silvery blade had fallen where they once stood.

"Are you OK?" Dale asked as he made his way over, the sight of where she had cracked three of the trees more concerning than his father's blade.

"Yeah, I'm OK you oaf. Do you know what that thing is?"

Dale turned back to the knife on the ground, his angel wiping away the leaves and twigs from her armor.

"No, should I?"

"If I'm correct, and my aching shoulder tells me I am, where I am from, they call it the 'Right Hand.'"

"The 'Right Hand' of what?"

Dale felt the tremors down at his feet as the small rocks rattled against the soles of his boots. The second tremor was stronger as it shook the ground at their feet enough that she grabbed his shoulder to help stabilize them both.

"Use your imagination, genius. The one thing I know is, wherever that thing goes, trouble follows."

The stars above them blacked out as a boiling mass of dark clouds rolled over the wooden walls. Water began to boil as the hydra climbed higher above the pool, its venomous teeth bared, and its limbs coiled back as the third tremor dropped both of them to their knees.

"Do you know how to fight?"

Dale couldn't answer before the gnarled barricade that separated them from the demons exploded.

* * *

"Run!"

Dale heard the angel scream before she evaporated into a ball of light and steamrolled into the darkness that fell over the opening in the wall. Wood logs and splinters littered the ground around him, the gap between their oasis and the world of the forest now gone as the hole was large enough to roll in an old Chevy truck.

Fear pushed him back as he stumbled to get to his feet. Fire lanced through his legs as he watched the arms of the hydra shoot out into the forest and coil around the shadows. Yelps of pain and damnation echoed into the night as the thorns bit into their targets.

The light and the sea creature were not enough. Demons poured in like a tsunami, their black mass a tidal wave of fear, and their evil magic leaving them featureless as the white light of his angel sparked and bounced from demon to demon.

Crawling backward, Dale could feel the stones in the dirt scratching at his skin. The creatures hadn't spotted him yet as the hydra and angel fought valiantly, though the certainty that they would find him cemented his feet to the ground.

"Get out of here while you still can!" Her voice echoed in his mind.

Water splashed on his back as dark masses fell into the pool. The bodies of demons floated by, torn and silent as the hydra bit one in half and shook its remains before throwing it back to the forest. Ghostly figures crawling on all fours climbed the serpent's body, scales and thorns falling as the beasts shredded its skin in any attempt to bring the defender down.

Dale could feel the beat of his heart as the blood pounded in his ears. Fear washed down his spine, the sensation leaving his limbs numb as he struggled to find the strength to move. Shouts and shrieks filled the night as rain started to trickle around the forest alcove.

In only a few moments, the sprinkle of water opened the heavens above as the rain began to fall in sheets and lightning streaked across the sky. Droplets trickled down Dale's face as he watched his angel's light continue to bounce through the darkness, its movements hard to watch, but the screams of her victims rang loud and clear.

He wanted to help; he wanted so badly to protect her as his dreams had told him to. What could he do? The evil that leaked from the demons was an ooze that covered him like a skin, its fear sinking deep into his soul as he could only watch in horror.

"Ah!"

Her voice crackled in his mind as her light tumbled across the opening and stopped with a thump against the tree line across from him. Cracks zigzagged their way up the wall as he watched her figure pull itself together from the light, her power struggling to continue the fight as she sprawled on the ground.

Blood covered her armor, black and oily as it stained her chest. Crimson red trickled down her forehead as he watched her face wince in pain as she pushed herself to her knees, the howls of darkness closing tightly around her. A large groan vibrated over the storm as he watched her regain her footing, the light of her power hesitating as her body started to transform.

Thrashing in the water behind him, Dale turned only a moment before that shredded corpse of a demon, bloody snout, and fire red eyes splattered at his feet.

"Oh my god!" Dale cowered as his legs kicked into drive and thrusted him backward.

Demon blood, salty and rank with iron covered his face as he stumbled onto his back. With a roll to the side, Dale felt his hand grip onto something that his mind had lost sight of, but the feeling of warmth flooded his soul the moment his skin made contact.

Light erupted through the forest as the shadows retreated in his vision. The cloud of evil disappeared as Dale's eyes widened to what he could see. Men, or what could once be called men, ran on all four limbs as they surrounded his angel. Their bodies were starved, the joints enlarged and grotesque from their transformation, but the dark power within them ate at their souls. Their red eyes burned as the demonic need for power consumed everything around them.

His angel continued to fight. He could see her graceful form tear into her enemies, her blade slicing through the demons like a hot knife through butter, but he could see her strength failing. Claws had torn her silk dress as dark stains wrapped themselves around her like the hands of a lover. There was no fear in her eyes as she pushed deeper into the enemy, her determination unending as the odds against her were too high for victory.

With a squeeze of the blade's handle, Dale pushed himself to his knees as he felt the presence behind him. Magic pricked the skin on his back, the tiny hands of the devil searching for a weakness it could use to take him. The demon sniffed the fear that cloaked Dale like an aura; it inched its way closer as the pounding of Dale's heart throbbed in his head.

Biting down on his lip, Dale spun and swung the weapon out in front of him like a shield as he fell backward. The demon reacted to the quick movement, clawed hands extended, Dale could see the transformed man's jaws open, and pointed teeth dripping with venom as it lunged forward.

Black magic exploded in front of Dale's face as the demon became a pile of ash the moment his blade made contact with its body. Flakes of burning embers floated to the ground, the essence of the evil magic dissipated as he pushed himself off of his back.

Seated, he watched as the fighting that surrounded his angel slowed. Those closest to her continued to fight, lunging through the opening and into the whirlwind that was her blade, hoping to take her down with numbers more than skill or weapons. Those furthest away had sensed the change the same moment Dale and the hydra that remained floating in the water did. They turned away from the threat that the angel imposed, allowing their attention to draw to him.

Dale could see the fire in their eyes. They looked at him, and he could feel their magic probe deep into his body where the seed of fear had sprouted. His weapon shook in his hands as he forced himself to his feet. Holding the weapon, he held the blade toward them. He didn't understand what it could do, or even how to use it, but the demons hesitated as they approached him.

Step by step they inched closer. Dark claws dug into the earth as they approached. Their elongated snouts lifted in the air as they inhaled the essence of the magic that Dale held in his hands. He could see saliva dripping from their jowls as they grew nearer. Six demons spread as they approached, each snapping their jaws as they remained far enough away to avoid the sword, but close enough he could feel their teeth tearing at his skin already.

Sweat ran down Dale's hands. He wanted to be sick. Blood covered him, and the stench of death filled the air. His knees were weak as he took another step backward; he didn't know how to fight, but he knew he couldn't allow them behind him. With each step, he tried to turn away from the pool of water where the hydra remained. If he fell, they would be on him. His throat was dry as the aches of his burning heart throbbed through his shoulders and down to the hands that gripped his father's gift.

"Ah!" Dale shrieked.

Pain scorched up his ankle as it turned sideways and tumbled him backward. The heel of his boot snagged on the vines that crafted his angel's tree stump seat and dropped him down, his back hitting the soft branches that created the backrest. All six of the demons growled excitedly, their eyes burning bright as they dug their claws deep and bunched their muscles to attack.

Swiftly, the line of demons swept to the side in a howl of anger as Learnie's arm wrapped around the first and dragged it across the ground and took the other five with it. All six tumbled together and crashed into the outer wall, yelps of pain rang out as the poison set in, but the evil would not be contained. Racing each other, five of the six climbed back to their feet and charged toward the pool of water. Their fight with Dale was forgotten, their anger and lust for blood turned toward the creature that had tattered their bodies with barbs and poisons that tore down to their bones.

Inching through the shadows, Dale watched as the darkness struggled with the light of his vision. He could see the carnage that laid around his angel, her form surrounded by the torn bodies of countless enemies that continued to stream from the forest. The Hydra, his male form hidden by his magic, struggled as the five demons danced around, their claws and fangs wearing the man and his serpent limbs down as blood and pieces of body floated across the water.

Dale let the tip of his father's sword touch the ground as he leaned against the trunk of the Oak tree that provided shade for his angel's bed. The only exit laid before him, filled with the bodies of a hundred dead demons, and it only led him deeper into the darkness that awaited them all.

Fatigue cramped his muscles. He couldn't move. He didn't want to move. Just yesterday his biggest worry was if there would be enough rain to grow anything but thistle in his village's garden. Now, he couldn't think of his life past the next few moments. His angel couldn't lose. She had been protecting his people for over ten years if his dreams had been true, but now he could see no way out. She was alone, and he was of no help. She would fight for them and watching as the blood of another demon splattered across the stained skin of her face, he knew she would die for them. But what could he do? He was only a young man, holding a blade he didn't even know how to use.

Squeezing onto the weapon's handle, he looked to the sky above. He watched the rain fall in gray droplets as another bolt of lightning streaked across the sky and slammed into a tree on the outside of the wooden barrier.

"Father, whoever you are, give me the strength to help. I do not have her courage, or her magic, but do not let her die this night," Dale pleaded into the darkness. "Give me some way to help her. Do not let us die out here in the dark."

Dale cringed as the taste of demon blood raced over the tip of his tongue. Iron and foulness choked in his throat, his stomach curling as the taste lingered in his mouth. The fighting was endless, the mass of darkness overwhelming the powerful light that filled his vision. He could feel the tears burn at the edges of his eyes as he fought the urge to crawl into a hole and hide. Maybe they wouldn't find him. Maybe this was all a dream.

A nightmare. He could live with that. He'd wake up in the morning and thank the heavens it was all over. The sword rattled in his hands as his legs struggled to keep him up. This night would be so much better if it were all in his imagination.

Dale squeezed his eyes as his heart skipped a beat. Thunder rumbled through the forest as the endless wave of demons parted, and the light of his angel remained. He could see her figure waver, the power of her light fading as she struggled to stand, her dress ripped to pieces, and her body covered in the gore of her enemies and her injuries. Moans echoed into the night as the man who was the hydra collapsed onto his knees, the bodies of demons scattered around him in the pool of water.

Steps. Colossal steps sent tiny earthquakes through the forest as darkness approached from the forest. Dale's new vision could not pierce the veil as the monster approached. The skeletons of Mother Nature's beauty only reached the chest of the enemy. It walked like a man, its shoulders hunched and layered with muscles. He could not see the head in the dark clouds above, but the red fire that ignited within its eyes shined like beacons into the night.

Lesser demons shrieked as the creature stood behind the wooden barrier. Sounds of fear and excitement raced through the night as the nightmare stood waiting as his angel remained resolute in her resolve. Dale couldn't breathe, his mind a blank slate as he stared at the thing that awaited them. It was death in physical form. No power nor angel could fight this creature. He fell to his knees as the tears rained from his eyes.

What could they do? Why did it have to be him?

He wanted to call out to her, scream her name before it was all over. But he didn't even know what it was. She was a mystery, a secret that would avoid him until the moment he died. His lips moved, and his lungs burned, but nothing came out as the darkness exploded around him.

* * *

"Why have you come here?"

Her voice struggled with disbelief. Dale could hear his angel, but his world was a dark void.

"It was you all along; everyone died because of you."

Who was she talking with? Dale struggled to move as pain wracked his entire body. He brought his hand to his face but could no longer see. He could feel his toes wiggle and both arms move, but the fear he was blind hit him like a speeding car.

The darkness. The evil had taken his sight.

"We trusted you!"

Her screams sliced into his eardrums as he rolled to his side. Coughing forced its way out as his eyes opened, and the shadows pushed back. He wasn't blind, but the smell of ash and dust filled his lungs.

"I should have killed you when I had the chance," her voice was trembling on the edge of fear and madness.

"Put all of this behind you. Join me and we can rule this world together," a male voice, deep and throaty answered.

Dale could feel his breathing struggle as he pushed himself to his knees. Dark soot rained from the sky as small fires burned throughout the forest clearing. The wall that had separated them all was shattered, broken limbs of trees smoked and lay scattered, the fog of destruction thick with despair.

"Rule this world?" Her words could not contain the madness. "He'll never let someone like you rule. You aren't strong enough to take his place. None of us are."

Dale pushed himself to his feet; he had rolled behind his angel's hammock when the explosion had rocked the earth. With his shoulder pressed against the remains of the oak tree, he used its faltering strength to keep himself upright, and squinted into the darkness.

Too much stood between them and him. They were dark silhouettes faded in the smoke that choked him every time he breathed.

"Do not mock me. I come to give you this choice freely." The demon's voice grew deeper with anger that rumbled with the threat. "The others were not as lucky as you are. Some I did not give a choice, some I did. They all chose wrong, and now you are the last of them. Do you want to perish like the rest?"

Dread washed over Dale as his knees buckled. He was going to kill her. His angel was going to die here and now, and then who would protect him, or his family? With a wobbly step, Dale inched his way forward through the shadows. Fires crackled behind him as he crouched to keep himself hidden. He didn't know what he would do, but he couldn't sit and wait.

With a step around the hollowed trunk of a tree, Dale could see a little more of what awaited him. His angel stood resolute, her light pulsing as she remained near what had been the barrier that kept the demons at bay. Blood covered her armor and matted her light hair to her head. Her shoulders were back; her chin pointed high though even from a distance of a few dozen yards he could see the freshness of the wounds that marked her body.

"I'll give you one more moment to choose, sister."

Dale's heart stopped with his breathing. Standing in front of her was the giant who had destroyed the wall and the demons that had breached it. His head was near the clouds; his wide shoulders tilted forward as he gazed upon the angel that was no higher than his knees.

With a hesitant step back, Dale felt his foot press down on something in the darkness. It wasn't a piece of burnt wood, nor was it the dry grass that had burned in the explosion. It was hard, and it resisted as it sank into the ground. With a turn to the side, Dale reached down and grabbed the object from behind the tree. It was his father's dagger, hidden from where it fell when he had toppled over the bed.

Light burst into his vision as the fires and smoke cleared away the moment he took hold of the weapon. The oasis was silent. The pool of dark water calm as the old man was nowhere in sight. His angel's powers pulsed in his vision as he turned toward her and the demon. She was once again in her silk dress, torn and bloody. She looked no better as the blood of her enemies mixed with the life that slowly drained from her.

The demon was different. He was no longer a giant, but a man only a head taller than she was. He was young, strong, and confident as he stood in front of the angel. Dark smoke emitted from behind the demon, as black as a starless night. The evil spread from his shoulder blades and opened like wings from his white three-piece suit with matching jacket, pants, and vest. His perfectly chiseled face with dark eyes and hair gazed down at her, his hands clasped at his waist as he awaited his answer.

Dale crept to the side, trying to leave as much between him and them as he could. The demon did not notice, his patience soon ending as the angel before him refused to respond.

"Will you defy me even now?" The demon opened his hands before clasping them behind his back. "After everything I have shown you, and even after watching you fight for your life, you deny my power?"

He could see the desperation behind his angel's eyes. Her face was strong, her lips a straight line of resistance, but she hesitated. Was she the last of her kind? Dale didn't know, and he wasn't sure he wanted to find out. The weapon in his hand shook like the leaves of a tree. Terror gave wind to his retreat as he found his way behind them, the former entrance the clearest path to the burning forest and the escape he desperately wanted.

"Come now, sister. Your last chance. What will it be?"

Dale had turned to run. Heeding her advice, he was going to make it to the path that led him back to his village. She had saved him. If he stayed, he would die. He knew she did not want that; she wouldn't have protected him if she didn't care. But why did his heart and soul scream at his first step away from the charred forest oasis? There was nothing he could do; this was his only choice.

"Do what you will. I will not join you, and you will fail!" his angel's voice screamed.

A high-pitched wail was muffled only a moment after it started as Dale closed his eyes to hold his tears as he began to run. Fear and anger burned within him as he pumped his legs as fast as he could. Eyes opened, there was no time for hesitation, no allowance for second thought, as he charged the demon with his father's sword held high over his head.

Sounds he didn't know he could make rolled from within him as each step brought him closer to the demon who held his angel by the throat with one arm. Dale's mind was gone, the horror of her limp body drove him mad as he pushed as hard as he could. If he died, it did not matter. She was all that mattered now. He had taken her from him, and he would not escape this forest.

Within two steps, the demon's empty hand darted out, open and aligned with Dale's throat as he ran right into its iron-like grip. Pain burned down the skin of his throat, and his chest burned with every breath. Dale pounded on the arm that now lifted him from the ground; his weapon dropped as he struggled to push the darkness that closed in on his vision.

"What is this here?" the demon asked, a look of amusement on his face. "A human this deep in the forest? I should have known she'd eventually fall from grace though you do seem a bit young for her. Pity, I always knew her tastes were a bit eccentric."

The demon tilted his head to the side, his eyes curious as Dale's arms weakened, his kicks no stronger than a toddler's.

"Tell me, boy. Is there anything special about you? Why don't you speak?"

Dale could feel his face burn as the tears ran down his cheeks. The fire scorched his insides as he no longer had the ability to fight, his arms and legs numb as his vision narrowed to a sliver.

"Weak. Father's imperfect children. We were supposed to worship you and bless you with gifts from the heavens. Look at you now. Pathetic." The demon spit as he lifted Dale higher, the red fire behind his eyes flared with intensity. "I will make an example of you boy, just before I wipe the rest of your village from the face of this earth!"

Thunder bellowed out of the demon's throat as his back arched, and Dale fell to the ground. Air laced with smoke and ash raced into his lungs as he coughed and struggled to stay awake. Light burst from the inside of the demon's jacket where the end of a dagger ripped through his vest. White light cracked through its skin as it struggled to turn, its power and strength failing as he continued to scream.

Dale backed away as the demon's eyes burst into the same white power that his angel possessed. The look of the demon's face was a mix of anger and shock as he gazed upon her beauty before he exploded and sent Dale tumbling backward.

No strength remained in Dale's arms and legs. It took all he had to look up from the ground, his mouth full of ash and dirt as his vision blurred. She was walking toward him, all womanly curves and white silk dress. He knew her; he knew what she was. Warmth filled his blood as she approached, and he could feel himself smile as his eyes closed.

* * *

"Feeling any better?" his angel asked.

Dale looked over at her. Her soft golden hair waved in the breeze as they looked down at his village below. He was feeling like a new man, his injuries gone and a confidence he had never known gave him strength. Three days had passed as he recovered in the small oasis. It had given her enough time to restore the balance that protected the clearing and the last bit of life within the forest.

She had trusted him with his father's weapon after informing him what it was. An angelic weapon, forged in the fires of Purgatory itself. She could not understand how he had gained possession of it. He had offered it to her, especially after they found Learnie, his serpent body torn by the explosion and scattered against the wall that had remained.

"You keep it. There is a reason you found it. Maybe one day it will lead you to who your father was."

Dale thought about that while he stood next to her. Her strength somehow bled into him. He was different now. Stronger, and for once he felt he had a purpose. Humans had a struggle ahead of them. A fight he wasn't sure they could win unless someone, somewhere, led them against the fallen angels and the demons that stalked what remained of humanity.

"Will I ever see you again?" he asked as he watched her from the corner of his eyes.

She smiled though she did not look at him.

"I will always be out here, just on the edge where your strength ends, and your beliefs begin." She paused as she looked up at the sky above, cloudless but with a blue that rang of hope. "Keep your faith, Dale. It served you well before, and it will serve you again when you need it most."

He smiled at that. Pride washed over him as he put his hands in his pockets and looked over his home. He would be going back with a story only he would believe. His journey had just started, but he would not forget her. His angel on the edge of his beliefs.

The End

Fish of the Dead

By
William J. Seymour
©2023

Detective Darkwater needs a new case. That means someone has to die. When Marina Coast Guard Rica summons him to Lightshire Pier, he knows that this case already smells fishy. What he doesn't know is how deadly the fish can be.

Work was slow these days. To some that might be a good thing, but for those who specialized in working with the dead, it made time drag by even slower. Especially when it didn't take a genius to know that eventually the bodies would start piling up.

They always did.

That was the good thing about the world. People enjoyed killing each other a little too much. It didn't matter if you were human, orc, goblin, elf, or any manner in-between. Death, murder, and violence all came naturally. No matter how much those priests carrying around books and waving burning incense tried to persuade you otherwise.

Today, was not one of those days. At least he hoped it would not be.

Fish, they stank both alive and dead. Anything and everything they touched picked up their odor and it's impossible to scrub it away. At the docks it was always worse.

The stench of the fish and the taste of the salt. Oil and lacquer mixed with unwashed bodies and too much bad rum. A stiff breeze from the west could never carry it away.

Detective Darkwater waited against one of the pilons that lined the pier. Three Keelboats sat anchored, and their cargo was in all states of unloading. Men gave orders as nets were pulled, boxes lifted, and the chaotic mess moved at its normal pace. A mix of endless traffic and never-ending work.

A single sailing boat, twin masted, sat at the far end, its pure white sales fluttering against the breeze that tried to pull it back out to sea.

Lightshire Pier.

One of two paths in and out of the city. The Sea of a Thousand Islands out to the east, the waters deep and dark, a place of merchant fisherman and travelers alike. The other, less traveled, is through the Mountain's Maw Pass. A month's passage through jagged peaks and glaciers that create a sea of their own. Land locked water, frozen and stretching for as far as anyone can see. One wrong unknowing step and it wasn't hard to find yourself falling to your death down a dark hole where there wasn't a soul around that would ever find you.

It makes this city the last stop for many a lost soul. The living graveyard unless you are willing to head back out to the unchartered ocean or to lands so unforgiving that ordinance required that all holdings within city limits be sold before venturing that way.

Everyone ignored Dark as he watched. His cigar pinched between his teeth, he took a deep breath and let the world move at its own pace. This wasn't a job for him. Times had been slow, but someone falling in the water drunk and washing up two days later was below his talents. Or the gods above be warned if it was some fight that got out of hand and one person ended up in the brig while one found an early nap below the ground.

He pulled the real mysteries, not your everyday crime that could be solved by following the simple trail of bad rum and mistreated women.

"A sight to see, isn't it?"

Darkwater turned. Coastie Rica Scarlog. Uniform pulled tight and trim, the marina guard was in perfect order as usual. Not a single strand of his dark hair was out of place and every line on his grey uniform with white trim was pressed solid.

The urge to straighten his own duster jacket found itself suddenly awake but faded quickly as he pulled from his cigar one more time and let it out before answering.

"Not my kind of thing," he answered, "but neither is being called to come and waste my afternoon."

The coastie nodded and took a step forward, his hands clasped behind his back as he took his position slightly ahead. Probably gave him a sense of superiority, but Darkwater said nothing. Some men needed that.

"From what I hear, business has been slow."

He nodded but decided to wait for the man to continue.

"To be honest with you, Detective, I'm not even sure this is a case for you."

"Then why did you even bother?"

The man's eyebrow raised. Darkwater waited for an answer, but it didn't take a genius to figure it out.

"Don't go there, Rica. Leave your sister out of this."

The coastie shook his head.

"She cares about you no matter what you want to believe. She's worried about your wellbeing. Things have been slow. The city guard has everything under control. When was the last time you had a case?"

"Last week they found a man impaled on a spike on the Peeking family estate," Darkwater answered.

Rica took a deep breath and let it out slowly.

"I heard it was one of their roofers who slipped because he had been drinking on the job. Pulled too many hours and fell when he left his lunch bag on a set of scaffolding. Inside was a half-pulled bottle of rum."

Dark turned back to the water where the sun reflected like a mirror and the waves broke across white crests before splashing against the pier. It didn't take a man of his talents to finish that case. Beneath the death and stench of ripped guts, the amount of alcohol that had been in his system was enough to take out a cow. Detectives don't get paid much for pointing out the obvious. They are there to see what others do not.

"Business has been slow. Things will turn around."

Rica put a hand on his shoulder and squeezed.

"For your sakes I hope you are correct. For the unfortunate bastards who have to die, not so much."

He looked at the man's hand and watched it slowly pull away.

"Doesn't explain why I am here."

Rica watched the business down by the pier for a moment in silence.

"Follow me. I want you to look at something. It might be nothing, it might be something. Only you can tell me."

"If it's nothing?"

The man pulled out a small bag of coin from his pocket.

"I pay you a day's wages for being here. But if it's something…"

"Then we see where the dead take us."

***

Fish.

Piles and piles of fish. Now he wasn't an expert on fish species, but these he had seen hundreds of times before and no one ever called them anything but 'white' fish.

Not exactly what he would call their grey scales and dead eyes, but he wasn't the expert here. After nights spent too long behind the bottle, he had taken the time to stare into the black depths hidden behind their deaths. A swirling pool that took him nowhere good. Memories he was happy to have blurred by the drink.

Today they stank and were limp and as cold as the iceboxes that stored them on the way back to shore.

The nets had dropped them unceremoniously on the pier and there was nothing left. Just three distinct piles of dead fish.

"Are you here to amuse yourself, Rica? Or did your sister beg you to throw anything you can at me, like charity to a beggar?"

Dark picked up one of the slimy specimens. The scales flaked away, and the lips had a spot of blood in the corner. Lifeless and gone.

Why was he here?

"Regardless of my sister's affection for helping lost causes, I would not waste my time any more than yours. This isn't about the damn fish, Detective," Rica answered.

Dark stood up, brushed his duster off, and regretted it the moment he did it. This smell was going to carry with him for hours, if not days.

The Keelboats were larger than they looked from the other side of the pier. At least sixty feet long, they bobbed on the water, their masts as tall and wide as trees as they creaked against the pull of their sails.

"I fail to see the reason I am here then. Dead fish are not my specialty."

He pulled a match and flicked it alight with the tip of his nail before putting it to his cigar he had regrettably let go out. The taste of the tobacco on his tongue helped push away the urge to toss the coastie out onto the water and go back to his office. It would be empty, but at least there was half a bottle whiskey waiting for him. The half he didn't drink when he bought it last night.

"We found them like this," a gruff voice said.

Darkwater turned.

Tall nor large was the way to describe the orc that looked down at him. At least seven if not eight feet of muscle and scars stared at him. Dressed in a simple cotton shirt that was open down to his navel, white lines ran all across the man's dark green skin, and his wool pants stretched at the seams to where his legs tried to force their way out. He kept a three-pointed hat on his head that tipped to the side to allow a long braid of hair to settle across his back. Six gold rings looped around the bottom where it ended at one hellish looking knot. His smile revealed one large tusk of a tooth that somehow found itself tipped in gold.

"And you would be?" Dark asked.

"Captain Gogron of the Shallow Isles."

The captain reached out a hand and Darkwater took it into his own. It made him feel like a newborn holding his father's hand for the first time. His bones ached from the thought that if the big brute wanted to, he could crush each bone into paste without hardly trying.

"I didn't think anyone from that place traded this far south."

The big orc crossed his arms over his chest, the material of his shirt stretching and showing off even larger scars along his skin.

"Business is business, and we have to follow the money. Many in these parts don't get the hauls we do, so I've made a good business providing."

"Until today that is," Rica added.

Gogron nodded.

Darkwater took a deep breath, the stench of the sea and the fish burned his chest more than the cigar did.

"I still don't see the purpose of my presence, Rica. Nothing against the captain here, but you need a warden or a sea-witch's help, not a detective. I'll take that payment, and I'll be on my way."

Dark bit down on his cigar, the taste a nice bitter note against the smoke that filled his lungs. He kept his hand in his pocket and waited on the coastie to offer the fee up before it became too apparent how little he really had.

"Explain it, Captain," Rica said. He pointed down at the pile of fish, still as unimpressive as it was before. "In terms our detective here will understand."

Darkwater sighed and looked back at the big orc.

"Fish dying after being caught, especially in large nets like ours is not uncommon, Detective. But I've never seen this," Gogron said.

He lifted one of the tiny corpses. Eyes glassed over, the blood at the corner of its mouth was black and salt dried.

"It's a dead fish," Dark said.

The captain tossed it over to him. Out of instinct he caught it.

"Open its mouth and look inside."

Darkwater looked back at Rica who waited without a word.

"All right, you get five more minutes. Then I'm forgetting I was ever here and I'm spending half of what you are going to pay me on an expensive lavender bath to get this stench out of my skin."

He pressed the corner of the fish's mouth and with a pop the lips opened. His eyes glassed over, and the world went dark around him as he looked inside.

Death.

Decay.

Rotted flesh wiggled and squirmed as the guts inside had liquified and the vile innards moved to find an escape. He could hear the voices calling to him. Dark words and names that should not be spoken.

Squeezing the fish, he let the tissue crack and decay until the corpse turned to dust and fell to the pier at his feet.

"All of them," Captain Gogron said.

Darkwater looked at him, then at the pile at his feet.

"That is why I called you, Dark. We have teams ready to burn them once you give us the go."

"My men have been sworn to secrecy, but it won't be more than a few days before the word gets out," Gogron added as he looked back at his ship. "Especially those here for their first trip. I have a tight grip on my men, but these ones seem particularly ill-equipped for this type of work. Hardly had the sea-legs to get here."

"This is some dark magic. Not your normal run of the mill wizard stuff."

"Then you'll look into it?" Rica asked.

He looked at the four ships anchored to the pier and back at the pile of undead fish at his feet. They all needed to be burned. The waters beneath swirled and foamed as the tide sang its rhythmic melody.

"Keep that bag of coins, Rica. You are going to need a lot more by the time this is done."

***

Three baths. Hot water filled with lavender and vanilla. It still wasn't enough. He could smell the stench on his skin. The fish smell that will never go away. Rancid and nightmare inducing. An invisible film between his fingers and under his nails.

All of it leaked from his pores. Its own poison that would carry with him for days. He closed his eyes and let his chin rest against his fists where he leaned forward over his desk.

A fire crackled behind him. Warm and inviting. He let the feeling sink into his bones, message its way through his muscles, and settle into the hollow spot within his chest.

Today's mystery had forced him to dig further into his notes than he intended for a day's work. Pages pulled from journals and books he would have rather kept up on the shelf collecting dust where they belonged. The vision from what he had seen and heard inside the fish played before his mind.

Those words.

Those names.

This area of the world had seen dark magic before, but nothing of this magnitude in a very long time. For him it hadn't been as long as he'd prefer, but he tried to make sure no one knew about that.

Before him sat everything he had on necrotic possession of amphibian forms. Zombie fish. Demonic sharks. Sea urchins that could eat a man whole. Monsters of the deep that fed on the living and worked with the dead. Rolled up scrolls and old books. Dust covered with pages torn around the edges from time's unforgiving hand.

He had writings on what sailors called the infamous kraken and everything in between that either really existed or were nothing more than drunken myths. Most people didn't understand how many of their nightmares were real, and those who did wanted to forget as fast as they possibly could.

"Did you find anything?" Hemley asked.

She looked at him with that grin on her face she always had. A tilted smile where very little of the darkness in this world could deter her pleasant disposition.

Many times in the past he had tried to push her off to some other vocation. A break from seeing the underbelly of this world. The fear ate away at him that if he didn't prevent it, it would darken even the brightest of stars, but she would have none of it.

The sun always rises to burn away the night.

She always reminded him of that fact no matter how much he tried to deny it.

"You've been at this for hours. Don't you think you should take a break?" she asked.

Placing a cup of hot coffee in front of him, her smile was even brighter as she wiped two loose strands of bright red hair away from her pointed ears. An elf wasn't an uncommon sight in this part of the world, but a highlands elf with their unmistakable bright hair and slender forms was noticeable no matter how much she tried to ignore it. Where men and women who worked the marinas and seas where browned to old shoe leather, Hemley's warm color came from years of riding horse in fields of grass and hills. It had a glow to it that spoke of youth and a life that had just started though he wondered how old she actually was. Elves and their long lives. She could be old enough to be his great-grandmother for all he knew.

Why she chose to spend her time in a city like this was anyone's guess. If it wasn't for her bright disposition and knack for turning even the worst of storms into a cloud with silver lining, he'd guess she had lost a bet and was here hiding from something dark within her past. Looking into her bright blue eyes, he wouldn't believe that if someone paid him all the city had in its treasury.

She sat down across from him. One leg crossed over the other and the tip of her long dark leather boot swayed its way back and forth. Even here in the city she always looked like she was ready to go out for a long ride.

"The captain said that the ship is setting sail first thing in the morning. I need to have everything I can ready before we set sail," he answered.

"You hate swimming, let alone the idea of being out on a ship. Plus, you already have business to take care of yourself here in the city. What made you take this job?"

"Professional curiosity. Wait, what business?"

His mind stopped as he tried to replay anything that had happened over the last week or two. Something that he was forgetting.

Her eyes narrowed and that smile of hers tilted into the most devious of grins.

"A Mr. Braco stopped by this afternoon before you returned. He said that you had an appointment with him, and you had missed it."

"Braco stopped here? He came here himself?"

Dark's heart would have raced if it didn't feel like it had already stopped. All the thoughts he had forgotten came rushing back. The money he owed. Debts unpaid since the jobs around the city had pretty much dried up. The thought of taking what Rica had already given him and catching the first carriage out of the city was a tempting idea.

"No, two men who said they worked for this Mr. Braco stopped by. I figured they were clients of yours and that you had forgotten to tell me about them. I put it down on your calendar, didn't you see it?"

He pushed away the papers and let a pile find its way to the floor. Right there in her handwriting. She even put a few circles around it with her elegant style of lite penmanship.

"Uh, yeah. I must have missed that. Did they say when they were coming back?"

"No, but they seemed pretty insistent that they see you. I told them I wasn't sure when you'd be back, but I promised I would get the word to you the moment I saw you."

"And I see that you have."

Dark looked around the room. The evening had spread its grip upon the city hours ago and there was little movement outside the window that looked onto the empty street. Late even for them to come calling.

Good, that would give him time to think of something. Braco wouldn't forget and if he had already sent two of his goons, then it wouldn't take him long to send them again.

"Maybe tomorrow. Afternoon at earliest. Possibly dinner time," he muttered to himself.

"What was that?"

He looked up at Hemley. She laced a lock of her hair around one finger and watched him as he absent-mindedly moved papers from one side of his desk to the other.

"Oh, nothing. If those men come looking for me again tomorrow, let them know they can tell Braco that I'll see him tomorrow. Late afternoon or dinner. If I'm not out on the water still when the evening comes. Can you remember that?"

She nodded her head.

"And the moon orchid only blooms at noon. What aren't you telling me, Shadow-Walker? You can always trust me. Maybe I can help."

Her name for him ever since they met. A traveler looking for a job in a city she had never been to before, he had run into her while working on the multiple murders of city guards who had run afoul of a ghoul created by a few local wizards in training who couldn't write let alone cast a proper spell to save their lives. Too bad their mistake had cost that of almost half a dozen others.

"Money is tighter than I like it to be," he said before turning his attention back to his books. "A small favor that I owe back to Braco. Nothing much. Rica already gave me a good down payment on this job, so I will settle things tomorrow."

"You sure I can't help?"

He didn't like lying to her.

"With what money? I hardly pay you as is, yet you stay here and work. Plus, it really isn't much. Enough for me to forget about as things finally roll in.

I'll take care of it. You don't worry those pretty little ears of yours.

"You are still no good at hiding things, but I'll leave this be. I may not have much in coin, but I could have a talk with this Braco if you want. See if he can hold off on any payments until you are back on your feet."

Dark felt his heart stop. The mere thought of Hemley getting tangled with the likes of Braco sent shivers down his spine. His hands went numb, and the back of his throat felt as dry as sandpaper.

"I've got this covered, Hemley. Forget Braco and this whole situation. Promise me."

The edge of her lip curled up into a devious little smile.

"So, if I'm not going to talk to your mysterious client, then when does our ship leave? First light?"

The words caught him by surprise.

"You aren't going. Someone has to stay here and watch the office."

To accentuate his point, he waved his arm around to the piles of books and notes that had yet to be catalogued.

"And all of that will still be here when we get back."

He growled and turned away from her, his attention on whatever paperwork he could quickly grab.

"There is no discussing this. My word is final. You will be staying here."

Somehow, he could still feel her smile even if he couldn't see it.

"Whatever helps you sleep tonight, because I know you will need it."

He growled again. Her steps were soft and almost silent, but he could feel her presence as she appeared behind him. Her hands on his shoulders were warm and gentle. Unable to stop her, she placed a kiss on the top of his head before she turned away.

"Good night, Shadow-Walker."

"Trouble sleeping my ass," he whispered to himself.

In the bottom drawer of his desk, he kept a bottle of whiskey that was now two thirds empty, but it was enough to take the edge off. He took a deep breath and closed his eyes. His mind was racing, and he needed to think clearly.

Those voices. Braco knocking on his door. It had been so long since he had heard them in this part of the world, and now he'd have to watch his back in every dark alley while dealing with this. A distant past that he wanted to keep that way.

Hundreds of fish. All of them dead at the same time.

What would kill so many and then bring them back to life?

No, not kill. Those fish did not die in those nets. There isn't a poison or parasite that could have done this.

He opened his eyes, twisted the top of the bottle and took a long, hard pull. The drink burned the entire way down and he didn't care that he couldn't even remember where the glasses were.

Yeah, she was right. Tonight, was going to be a long night.

***

Seagulls squawked even this early in the morning. Off to the east the dark sky presented an almost unnoticeable lightening, but men were already hard at work. The boat swayed and everything still stank of fish and unwashed bodies. A day on shore was not enough to help.

Darkwater leaned over the railing of Captain Gogron's ship 'Night's Mistress', his eyes watching the ripples that formed around the boat's hull. Leaves and trash of discarded food and other belongings floated around with the bubbles as the ship remained at anchor. They'd be going out once all their gear was stowed away. A voyage that would take them out to where the fish had been caught. He didn't really like it, but it was better to look in case anything was missed.

"I hope you can handle the trip," Captain Gogron said.

Dark looked over. The big orc stood tall without a single look of exhaustion this early in the morning. He was certain the captain purposely purchased clothes that were too small for a frame like his. The seams looked ready to scream along the edges of the new cotton shirt and pants eerily similar to the ones he wore the other day.

"Why would you ask otherwise?"

A smile broke the captain's face.

"Because I may have mentioned the story of what happened the last time you were on a ship," Hemley said as she stepped out from behind the big orc.

"Rather amusing tale if you ask me," Gogron added. "Don't you worry. We'll get you some sea legs soon enough, or we'll toss you out with the fishes."

The captain laughed as he walked away, leaving him with Hemley.

"Didn't need to tell him about that," Dark said as he looked back down to the water.

"Just trying to loosen the crew up a little. See if there is any information we can get out of them," she said.

He looked over at her. The smile on her face never went anywhere, even if he could see her eyes surveying everything. He would never admit it to her, but he was glad she had come along. Maybe a tad boring, but better spent with her than with a bunch of full-grown orcs who probably haven't spent a full day with a man of the city in their lives.

"Get anything out of them?"

She shook her head.

"Nothing more than we already have. The fish were picked up like we saw them. Dead, yet still alive."

"And none of them saw anything out of the usual? Did you ask if any of them had seen magic of this sort before? Maybe something from their home back in the Shallow Isles."

She put her hands on her hips and tilted her head.

"You act like this is the first time I've come along on one of your jobs. But no, not a mention of anything of that sort. Some mentioned that they thought they saw another boat out on the water where they were, though they weren't the most forthcoming."

Dark's interest finally peaked enough to take his mind off the rocking on the boat.

"Why would you say that?"

She shrugged.

"A lot of them mentioned that Captain Gogron made it explicit that they are not to talk to anyone. The few who let it slip did so in passing. My guess is that their fishing route is as secret as we thought, but possibly not secret enough to be known only to them."

"Seems the captain forgot a few more things than he let on."

She nodded her head and turned to look out at the churning water.

"Then we are no better off," he finished. "A job possibly dealing with a death magic I haven't seen before, and a captain who is already keeping secrets."

"Would you really expect different?"

Hemley leaned on the railing and let her shoulder press against his. He could smell the light touch of lavender in the air around her and pulled the smallest smile to his face. Only she could find a way to push away the stench of dead fish and the sea.

Gogron called out and the lines were pulled from the pier, the ship bucking as the sails caught and pulled them with a jerk.

"No, I wouldn't have expected anything less," Dark answered as he caught his balance with a grip on the railing that turned his knuckles white.

Hemley chuckled and rubbed his shoulder with one hand.

"Worse thing that happens is we spend a little time out on the water if what he is hiding stops us from finding anything. Anyway, you could use a bit of sun and time away from the city," she added as they put more and more distance between them and land.

He looked back at the marina and the rapidly receding city. It had been a very long time since he had ventured out of the city limits, but he wasn't certain a few days out on the water was the worst that could happen. Never seemed to be the case every time he let himself stray too far from his own territory.

"Did you happen to see when any of the other ships left port?" he asked.

"You think we might catch a glimpse of the one they claim may have found their route?"

Dark shrugged. There was little to see as the waves broke against the hull and they road the waves. Hemley shook her head.

"Captain said two of the other fishing boats were gone late last night, picking up anchor before the local pubs even cracked their second barrel."

He turned back to the marina where only one remained.

"What about that two-sail pleasure boat? The one that looked more like a personal yacht than a workman's job?"

She shrugged with her eyes locked to the horizon.

"No one mentioned anything about seeing that one. Wasn't here when I arrived at first loading."

Hemley sat herself down on the railing, her feet kicking back and forth as she closed her eyes and let the wind run its way through her hair.

"Seems odd so many people rushing to be back out on the water. Especially if they aren't catching anything but dead fish."

"That's why we are here, Shadow-walker."

He ran his hand through his own thinning hair, the cold bite of the sea breeze sending a shiver down his spine.

"How's that?"

"You see what others don't. The oddities and the unusual. All that is hidden in the shadows that the common folk don't know or want to know about."

She let herself drop back down to the deck and slid up beside him.

"And what about you? Why are you here?"

"Because you are horrible with paperwork and paying your bills."

Her arm slid beneath his elbow, and she pulled herself tight against him.

"Now, let's go have another conversation with our captain, why don't we?" she asked as she led them both toward the cabin where most of the crew waited for the work to begin.

***

No wind. Unbroken water. The smell of rotten, stagnant water. It was more swamp than ocean. Flotsam and debris bobbed across the surface. Broken crates. The top of a mast that had snapped not far from the crow's nest.

They had arrived. The middle of the sea. The middle of nowhere.

Water turned to nothing more than a dark looking glass for as far as they could see, yet nothing to explain the debris and the carnage. Dark could feel every tiny rock of the boat in his stomach. He refused to look at any of the crewman. Their voices, hushed whispers, carried easily and it was all at his expense. Little jabs and harsh jokes. He bit down on his lower lip and refused to let his guts spill out over the edge. Again.

Green water, covered with film and bits of passing debris, foamed along the hull's edge. He could smell the rot, but more importantly the magic. It wasn't only life that lived below the water's edge. It was the entire area. Diseased and worsening.

The clear sky beat down on them and made the smell worse as if they had sailed right into the middle of a garbage pit.

"Wasn't like this the last time we passed through," Captain Gogron said.

His yellow eyes squinted at the sun, the bright rays glistening against his dark green skin. He still had his hat on, but the shirt had left hours before as the heat grew with every passing minute.

"So, all of this is new?" Hemley asked.

The captain nodded.

"Wouldn't fish here if the water stank this bad. Looks more like a battle that ended for everyone involved. Nothing would live out here. Wouldn't want to eat anything that did."

Dark looked at him then back at the water, the sudden movement of his head spinning his vision. After confronting the man once the city was out of sight, he had admitted to telling his men to be less forthcoming even with the detective. When questioned about the possible other boat, he had proven less reliable saying that he hadn't seen it himself and doubted others did as well. Their route and most successful drop spots were well kept secrets that only he and a few others knew. Coming from some of his greenest men, their imaginations probably took a hold of them once the zombie fish were pulled aboard.

"I wouldn't want to eat anything out of here either. Everything is lifeless," he said.

The captain nodded but Hemley had her eyes out on the horizon.

"Do either of you see that?" she asked.

They both looked. Far out beyond range, they couldn't make out clearly, but there appeared to be two pointed triangles breaking the surface of the horizon.

"Shark fins?" Dark asked.

They'd have to be the largest sharks he'd ever heard of to be seen from this distance, but the way they broke from the surface of the water at the edge of their vision was not natural.

"Give it a moment," Gogron said.

Their eyes remained fixed as the boat continued to bob in the water and whatever it was off in the distance grew closer.

Bright white against the beautiful blue where the sky dipped beyond the level of the sea. Moments passed like hours and more and more of the ship's sails came into view. Within moments they could see enough to recognize the ship that had been at port the prior night.

"I'm guessing that would be the ship your men claimed they saw, Captain," Dark said.

The big orc took a minute, his eyes concentrating on the new arrival.

"Very few sail these seas, Detective. It is how I make my living. Too many rumors about where I come from. Keeps strangers and merchants away."

"Shallow Isles," Hemley added.

Dark gave her a glance but turned back to the captain.

"Wonder why they are out here then."

They all stood there as time passed. Their new fishing buddy drew no closer as if they'd dropped anchor right where they were.

"Do me a favor, Captain," Dark broke the silence.

The helmsman turned his head, but his eyes remained on their silent follower.

"Cast a net like you normally would. Pull it up and let's see what you catch."

"Here?" asked Hemley.

"Curiosity. Everything should be dead, correct? The waters here are putrid. See what your nets catch."

The captain nodded, but his attention hardly wavered from their strange visitor. The rocking of the boat and the tap of a rope against the central mast finally broke the spell as he barked a few commands at his fellow sailors. Within moments the lines were dropped. Dark turned back to the strange boat and watched as the ship remained right where it was. No matter how far they drifted, the other stayed right where they could see little more than the sails.

What are they doing here?

"That's it men, pull it on up," the Captain barked.

Dark greenish water splashed onto the deck and the smell of rotten flesh and dead fish hit them all like a punch to the gut. The railing was all that prevented Dark from throwing himself overboard with the heaves of his guts as what little remained inside of him emptied into the sea.

Men yelled, their words lost to the confines of his nausea. Dark gripped the rails with all his might, the need to heave everything so strong the world spun before his eyes.

"They're alive!"

He heard the voice, but it felt like it was miles away. The sky turned dark, clouds ran in, and the wind picked up and threatened to turn the boat over. Rain pelted his face and he squinted against the burn of the salt. More shouts. Everything was lost. This was the end of the world. They would all die here, sunk to the bottom of the sea.

"Shadow-walker! They are alive!"

He felt her words more than heard them. Hemley. She shook his shoulders, and he opened his eyes. The sun was still up, bright and burning high in the sky. The stench of fish was heavy with the mix of death, but the entire deck was covered in flopping fish. Grey scales glistened as the things bounced around in dire search of the water needed to keep them alive.

"Get…get me one," he struggled to say while wiping away the drool from his lips.

She gave him a hard look, then turned to the men already picking up the catch.

"Here! Toss me one of those."

The nearest sailor did as he was asked. The fish flipped in mid-air where she caught it without hesitation.

"See, they are alive. Even in this poison the fish still live," she said with the biggest smile on her face.

Dark shook his head. He reached out and she placed the slippery thing into his open hand. His guts turned and a cold bolt of lightning ran through his veins like a razor-sharp knife. The words he had so long ago struggled to forget came rushing back to his mind. The world turned grey before his eyes. Hemley, her beautiful face and ageless features wrinkled and decayed before him. Men all over the ship shriveled as flesh melted off their bones and their skulls sunk in to reveal hideous faces wrought with fear and anger.

He turned the fish toward him, its maw opening and closing as the thing slowly choked to death. Inside the guts had liquified and maggots grew where the flesh rotted. Disease and death swirled in tiny green circles and the voices from within the bowels called out the screams of the damned. He dropped it from his hands, the wriggling form bouncing between his knees where he sat.

"They are all dead. Every single one of them," he choked out, his mouth full of bile and the taste of acid.

"What do you mean? That's not possible," she said.

With uncanny ease, Hemley picked up the fish. She turned it over and looked inside. With a gasp she turned back to the pile the was quickly being cleared by the sailors.

"Throw them overboard!" she yelled. "All of them. Back into the sea."

The men stopped. Without moving they turned to Captain Gogron who only nodded. Without a word of complaint they did as they were told. Bucket after bucket of the undead things were dumped back into the putrid waters. Dark could not find the strength to stand, the words vibrating in his head enough to split his skull. Shifting what he could of his weight he turned back to the front of the ship, the gaps between railings giving him enough to see.

Empty.

The horizon was empty. Their silent stranger was no longer in sight.

****

Stars filled their world. The sky and across the city. Thousands of them danced along the waves of the black glass that filled the marina. Dark watched where the docks, the streets of the city, and the piers along the water burned with torches and lamps that filled the darkness with eyes at all corners.

"Hell of an adventure this trip was," Captain Gogron said as he slapped him on the shoulder.

Dark stumbled a step forward, but his returning strength helped him stay upright. Without missing a beat, Hemley placed her arm beneath his elbow and leaned against him as the ship came to rest against the pier.

"Something like that, Captain. What are you all going to do now?" he asked.

The captain gave him a long hard look.

"A few days shore leave won't hurt the men. Probably spare them all a few coins from what they would have had if the catch had been a success."

"You're a good man," Hemley said.

"I try my best, young lady. They work hard, though times have been rough. I can afford to give what I can, but if this doesn't turn around, we'll be headed back to the isles without much hope of any return."

Dark stopped, stiffened his back as much as he could and looked the big orc in the eye.

"I'll do what I can, Captain. Something is happening out in those waters, and I intend to figure it out before you and your men have to break port. Be safe while you are here. I will check in with you as soon as I can."

The big captain nodded and shook his hand.

"You'll know where to find us," he said and turned back to his ship.

Large strides carried him back as if he didn't have a care in the world.

"That's a big promise, Shadow-walker."

He looked at Hemley.

"Someone has to help, and the local authorities won't be of any use."

She smiled as they both turned away from the large fishing vessel and started to walk back into the city.

"What?" he asked.

"Nothing," she giggled.

"Tell me or I'm not going anywhere."

They stopped and she turned to look him right in the eye.

"You've got an idea already. You've figured it out," she said with a devious giggle.

Her teeth nibbled on her lower lip, and she ran a finger over the outside of his jaw. He took her hand in his and slowly pushed it away.

"Not in the least, but I'm certain of only one thing."

Shaking his head as if suddenly remembering where he was, he turned and headed across the marina instead of away.

"What is that?"

The captain's boat was tied to the pier where it was before, the last in a line of ships that had dropped anchor at the city. Four more fishing boats had arrived and at the end was the one he was looking for. Two masts, all white and bright even in the fading light.

"Our visitor has returned before us," he said as he kept his eyes on the dock that led to the large pleasure boat.

"How is that?"

"No ports for oars, only two masts. That is a terrific question. How did they make it back before we did with a full crew of strong orcs at the oar?"

She nodded her head but did not mouth the words.

"I think we should find out."

Taking her hand, they both walked along the marina. Merchants and sailors pushed their way along, many carrying loads fresh from the sea and others barked orders of where things were to go and how much was being paid. Others, long hard looks of dead eyes and hungry bellies, begged for work, their bodies long past the ability to pull in the labor they promised.

Dark did what he could to push their way though, the crowd thick like snow in the dead of winter.

Their destination glowed white in the dismal surroundings of the pier. The sailors that stood outside wore uniforms, tightly tailored to their bodies, of the most brilliant of white. Singular pointed caps of seamen sat atop their heads and their training stood through as they watched everyone around them, yet their eyes did no move. Their muscles flexed and relaxed beneath the tight uniforms as the voices rose and fell around them.

"Is the captain available?" Dark asked as he reached the first two who stood at the edges of the pier.

They hardly spared him a glance.

"My name is Detective Darkwater. I am investigating circumstances that have fallen upon some of your fellow sailors within the city. I ask again is your captain available?"

Neither man broke their silence. Hemley squeezed his arm, and he returned a tap on her hand.

"Well, if neither of you feel the need to answer I shall return with Coast Guard Rica. Maybe then you'll be able to answer my questions."

Still no response. Pulling Hemley closer, he turned to go find Rica, wherever the damn man happened to be at this time. This was becoming more of a problem, and it was going to require more than a title to get him where he needed to be.

"Ah, Detective! Don't be so hasty to leave!" a man's voice called from the ship.

Dark and Hemley turned, both guards now standing sideways leaving a wide lane up the pier. Walking quickly down the ramp that led up to the ship's deck was a portly fellow dressed in what had to have been his nightclothes. Pants and shirt of light pink silk, his shoes were made of the fluffiest fur Dark had ever seen, and the glass he carried in his hand was more than half empty. The fellow waved as he stepped onto the pier like they were old friends and tried not to trip over his own soft shoes.

"Please…please excuse these two gentlemen. Where they are undeniably the best at following orders, they tend to lack social skills. That is what you get for putting your coin where your mouth is sometimes. Please, would you join me back on the ship for a drink?"

The alcohol was easy to smell beneath the salt and the fish brine already in the air. One leg slightly shorter than the other, the man already looked tilted to one side, but this was probably going to be easier than finding Rica beneath his own drinks and dragging him out here in the middle of the night. Their new friend had a genuine smile beneath his bushy mustache and his eyes were bloodshot behind one too many drinks.

"We would both love to," Hemley interjected.

Dark shot her a look, but her full smile was easy enough to read.

Be quiet and follow my lead.

He nodded and the jolly man tried to clap his hands together, some of the drink within his glass spilling.

"Excellent. Please, follow me."

Tapping one of the men on the shoulder, he led them up the pier and then onto the ramp. Upon closer inspection, the magnificent ship was not as pristine as it had looked from a distance. Cracks ran deep spidery lines over the white outer coat. The railing along the deck was moldy at the joints and the wood cracked with sun and salt. Floorboards creaked as they stepped onto the deck and the light around them was a dull firelight orange from lanterns that hung on pegs around the cabins at the center.

"Are you the captain of this ship?" Dark asked.

There were three other sailors onboard where he could see. One at each end and the last atop the cabins, their stances keeping them at attention and their uniforms cleaner than the vessel they guarded.

"Oh, by the gods, no," the man answered. "By the way, my name is Doctor E.Z. Conven. I am what… what would you call?"

He waved his drink in the air, his eyes and lips trying to catch words that were nowhere to be found.

"A drunk?" a woman's voice asked from within the cabin.

The doctor snapped his fingers.

"I am a researcher! Though I may have had one too many tonight!"

He saluted them with his drink as he stepped to the side.

"May I introduce you to the captain of this magnificent vessel, the Lady Alexa Knob."

Conven bowed, what little he had left to drink spilling onto the deck. Stepping out of the cabin, a woman dressed in the finest of silks Dark had ever seen, the Lady Alexa was not what he was expecting. Tall, beautiful, yet not young. There were years behind her eyes, dark and full of knowledge he could recognize even in the dimming light. Her smile was short, a courtesy at best, and her long dark hair was laid back where it fell just beyond her shoulders. The white silk of her dress was like that of her sailors, pristine and spotless.

"My lady," Dark said with a bow.

Hemley gave a slight bow as well.

"Ah, Detective, I have heard so much about you," she said in return.

With a wave of her hand Conven backed away and vanished back into the cabins.

"You have?" Dark asked.

He looked over at Hemley who returned her own confused look.

"Nothing but good reports, I assure you. I was wondering how long it would take for you to come and make my acquaintance."

Taking Hemley's hand in his, he pulled ever so gently until she was forced to take a step behind him. He could feel the eyes of the men who guarded this ship on them. There was only one way off this boat and even if they did make it off, the pier was blocked unless they jumped into the water. This did not leave them many options.

"Why would you think that?"

He squeezed her hand and was glad to feel her squeeze back.

"You're investigating the undead fish our orcish friends from the Isles have been catching. Hard to make money selling things that still swim long after death has taken them."

"So…what do you know about them?"

Her smile grew.

"All in due time, Detective. Come in, let's have a drink together, and I'll tell you all I've done already to stop it."

***

There was a glamour about everything within the cabin. Exquisite white serving plates sat on a table seated for four. White linens with matching silverware and sparkling crystal glasses finished the setting. The room itself was brighter than a few well-placed lanterns alongside the windows should have allowed.

Dark could feel the magic in the room. It hung like a mist. Sticky to the skin, it gave the room an almost electric taste. Lady Alexa was the first to sit, Conven quick to pull her chair out and help her find a spot. Hemley hesitated, her eyes searching, but when Conven offered her a seat, she took one as well. Dark remained standing, his hands resting on the back of Hemley's chair.

"You said you have been working to stop what has been happening already?" he asked.

Her lips curled at one corner, and she took a moment to settle herself in her chair once more, one leg crossing over the other and her long fingers smoothing out her dress before taping along the top of the table.

"Would you like something to drink first? Maybe a bite to eat? I gather you may be hungry after such a voyage. Tends to turn the stomach when you aren't accustomed to such a trip."

Dark looked down at his shirt, a few white spots dribbled across the material from where he had gotten sick. To be honest, he felt lucky it wasn't worse.

"I'd rather discuss what we have come here for and then be on our way. As you said it was a long voyage and an equally long day."

She nodded and lifted a finger.

"Conven, please find me a good vintage stored down below. I have a feeling I may be a bit parched after the detective and I are done here." Conven bowed and vanished out a door at the back of the room that led to a set of stairs deeper into the ship. "So, where were we? Ah, yes, what I have done so far on our exploration of the zombie fish."

"Zombies?" Hemley asked in feigned shock.

Her eyes were wide and looked to him for explanation. There were still too many questions and not enough answers, so he shook his head ever so slightly and placed his hand on her shoulder.

"Is that what they are?" he asked in return.

Lady Alexa's smile grew more devious as she eyed Hemley.

"You can't fool me, Detective. I've heard enough of the stories and done plenty of my own research to know you are more than meets the eyes. Out on those waters the stench of necromancy is as pungent as the salt itself. There is no denying you can feel it even before you see what repercussions it brings. Then there are the fish themselves. Still moving weren't they. Alive as ever until you look at them."

Dark let himself find a seat at the table. His hands clasped together.

"Tell me what you know. Very few understand anything at all about magic of that sort, let alone have the ability to recognize it."

"Even fewer know how to practice it," she added.

Conven returned with an unmarked dark green bottle, popped the cork and poured the deepest red drink Dark had seen in ages. He could smell the wood smoked berries from where he sat.

"Still doesn't explain your efforts in all of this."

She took a long sip and swirled the crystal in front of her eyes.

"A good choice, Conven. Well, Detective, how much do you know about your orc friends?"

Dark let himself rest against the back of his chair. He looked over at Hemley who stayed silent, but her gaze continued to travel around the room.

"I wouldn't call them friends. The Coastal Guard Rica brought me in. I have a history with him and his family. He said he had some work for me and that I'd get paid regardless if I could help or not. Then he introduced me to Captain Gogron and his crew. Nothing more, nothing less."

"It didn't concern you that you'd be paid regardless of your efforts? A man of your talents and…debts."

A spike of ice shoved its way through Dark's heart, but he couldn't let her see that. Instead he shook his head. Inside he knew that he wasn't going to like where this was going to go.

"None of which should concern you. Like I said, the Coastie and I go back. Family business. We tend to look out for one another."

She nodded and took another sip.

"Very well. I'll fill you in on some things. Captain Gogron and his crew are not your average men who bring trade to this port or any port."

Dark crossed his arms over his chest.

"They are ship full of orcs coming from the Shallow Isles. Not your everyday thing in the land of man. Doesn't mean there is anything wrong with them."

"Very progressive of you, Detective, but that is none of my concern either. What I mean is they are good at what they do. Some accuse them of cheating other merchants. Stealing from them. Raiding ships. Taking what isn't theirs and then selling it as if it was their own. They are very successful merchants, wouldn't you say?"

"I didn't sense that in any of the men," Hemley chimed in.

The expression on her face was of concern and shock. As if Lady Alexa had just personally insulted her mother. Dark squeezed her hand, the muscles in her face relaxing at the touch.

"Those who lose anything, let alone business, to those unlike them are prone to fantastical stories. Lies even. I didn't see any evidence out on the water while I was with them. The men were well trained and professional. Not exactly the type to be pirating ships for expensive cargo."

"Plus, the dead fish means they get no money. Are you saying they stole the fish off someone else's ship, then brought them here?" Hemley added.

Lady Alexa shook her head and held up her glass for Conven to refill.

"What I am saying is these friends of yours have not made many friends. Either via honest trade or not, they are not liked nor wanted in these parts."

"So, let me read between the lines here. Someone is using necromancy to ruin the business of Captain Gogron and his men. Cause them to lose enough money on these trips and they'll never come back."

The mysterious woman nodded her head.

"See, Detective. I knew it wouldn't take much for you to catch on."

"Not exactly a far stretch of the imagination. But that brings us to you and your involvement in all of this. How do you explain that particular piece of information before we even go into who has the ability to pull something like this off."

With a deep sigh the woman put her glass down and sat forward, her elbows touching the table and her chin resting in her hands.

"Let's consider it a good Samaritan gesture for free trade at our port. Like you, Detective, I am not without my own abilities in these matters." She waved one hand to the cabin around them, her eyes boring into his. "Many who dabble in the arts are capable of both good and evil. It is all about how it is done and who gets to be the judge."

"And I am to trust in both your judgement and to take your word for this."

She tipped her glass toward him, the corner of her mouth hooking.

"Exactly."

As the crystal touched her red lips, Dark felt a shift in the room. A waver in the glamour that coated the cabin, the boat, even the occupants. Darkness and age flashed as the curtain was pulled back and he could see what the world really was.

Hemley beside him did not move, her stoic look rock solid as she continued to monitor everything around them.

Cracks and splintered boards held the ship together. The linen that sat upon the table was wrinkled and worn at the edges, a dark stain sitting beneath where Captain Knob rested her glass.

Then she winked her eye, and a burst of power rippled its way through the cabin and out across the ship.

"Is there anything else I can help you with, Detective?" she asked.

Hemley turned to him, a questioning look on her face.

Dark took in the magic around them and the little information she had been actually willing to share. There was nothing else he was going to learn, at least here.

"Not at the moment, Captain. I thank you for your hospitality," he answered.

She did not rise as he and Hemley stood from the table. Legs crossed, she took another sip from her glass and Conven escorted them out.

***

The glamour returned to full effect. The door shut softly with a click and the sound of the waves as they broke against the pier filled the night air. The city was asleep, the murmur of thousands of voices carried through the day dimmed down to a soft hum.

Hemley kept her hand in his, a squeeze every few moments as they stood there outside the cabin. Along the railing and down on the pier the men still waited, their arms locked behind them as they stood at attention.

"So, what are you thinking?" Hemley asked.

He did not look at her. Instead, he kept his attention on the water, a darkness so solid he could not tell where the sea ended, and the sky started.

"Follow me," he said, his words hardly more than a whisper.

They walked hand in hand down from the vessel to the pier and past the men who stood watch. Everything had returned to the way it was supposed to be. Flawless white paint that gave the ship a glow even in the darkness, all signs of age and use gone. He could feel the pulse of the magic that sustained the illusion. There was an ebb and flow to it, but the force behind it had picked up, no chance that flaws would break through now that they had left it behind.

"Are you going to say anything?" Hemley asked.

They walked along the marina, the large ships reduced to dark shadows that danced in the swaying light of lanterns and watched by dark eyed men with gruff looks and the smell of alcohol on their breaths.

"I don't trust her, but we have less to go with if we excuse her words as pure opportunistic chance. We need to dig a little deeper."

"How are we going to do that?"

They reached where the ship from the Shallow Isles remained docked.

A single lantern hung from the cabin; no sight of a watchman posted anywhere near the vessel.

"We are going to go find our good men, wherever they happen to be. For people who seem to be not well looked upon, and worried that they will be forced to return home empty handed, they sure have little regard for the safety of their ship."

Hemley followed his gaze to the vessel. Nothing moved that they could see. An empty fishing boat left to sit the night.

"How about I go back to the office and see if I can find some contacts here at the marina. See if they know anything about the history of Captain Gogron and his men. The success or lack there of when it comes to their business."

Dark nodded his agreement.

"That is a fine idea. I'm going to go find the captain himself. Make sure he and the others are keeping themselves safe this evening."

She squeezed his arm with hers one more time.

"You'll do the same for yourself, correct?"

Her eyes were soft in the orange glow of the lantern light and the smile that was forever on her face was missing.

His words were lost within that look for a moment.

"Yes. I will be extra careful. I don't exactly hold the same apprehension about the fate of our good captain as the Lady Alexa does, but I do believe something is going on here, and it pertains to a magic far more real than anyone wants to believe."

"If you need my help, you come and find me. Promise me."

She grabbed both of his elbows and locked her eyes with his.

He couldn't help the smile on his face.

"Absolutely. Now, be off. I have some orcs to find."

Her smile returned. She leaned in and kissed him on the cheek. Without another glance she spun on her heels and was into the shadows of the night in a matter of moments.

He stood there watching as the ships rocked with the moving tide. His mind swirling with so many questions.

Seagulls squawked and he snapped out of it. Turning, he headed away from the marina. It was not a long walk to the nearest watering hole. Sailors and their sea legs that did not carry them far when back on land. After a day out on the water, he could feel at least a little sympathy for the plight.

The smell of stale ale and the carrying of voices met him before the street did itself. Angry voices with threats lost amongst the growing chorus. Men stood outside watching through the windows.

Dark picked up his pace. The threats grew more distinct the closer he got. He could feel the tension in the air roll out of the alehouse like a fog.

"Excuse me," he yelled.

The men crowding around for a glance hardly noticed he was even there.

"Get out of my way in the name of the coast guard," he shouted again as he pushed his way around the heavy bodies of those that blocked his way.

Inside the stench of alcohol and dirty men almost took him off his feet. Everyone had grouped into a circle, a gathering of animals waiting for the slaughter.

"You'll eat those words you mouth breathing pink ear!" one of the men in the center threatened.

Dark struggled to make his way toward the combatants. No one wanted to give him more than a hair's width of room. The excitement had swallowed them whole and the need to see blood sank its teeth into their own primal instincts.

"Your disgusting kind shouldn't even walk these streets, let alone this world. We'd all be better off if your boat sank on its way out of port," threatened another.

More voices tried to prod each of the men on. Threats added upon threats. Dark struggled to squeeze through before this turned into total mayhem.

"We make better sailors than any of you scum. Our catch makes all of you look like little boys with fishing rods. How about you take your ship and find something good to do with it, like drive it into the local shallow reef. I heard your pretty good at doing that."

"At least what we catch is still alive. Your kind is trying to poison us with the disgusting stuff you've been trying to sell. We've all seen what has been coming from your nets."

Dark let his ears catch on to that. None of those fish were ever taken from the ship, the presence of the zombified catch held to those of the crew and the guard itself.

"I'm going to kill you!" the man from Captain Gogron's crew yelled.

Dark was too far away to reach them and stop the bloodshed himself, but he couldn't let one of the crew go to the local jail, nor lose what sounded like his only real lead.

The lights faded to a light grey and his blood turned cold as he dug deep within himself. Voices filled his ears, chants that vibrated through his bones as the icy fingers of death ran along his spine. His lips moved, the taste of bile swirling around his tongue, and he pushed the power from his fingertips to the ground at his feet.

Black smoke pulled its way up through the floorboards, hands of gray reaching up as they tugged at the pants and legs of everyone around him. With a twist of his wrist and a tap of his fingers he sent the necrotic circle of the damned forward. Everyone in front him took little more than a moment to start to buckle as the magic took hold.

Men gurgled and began to choke. The strength drained from their bodies as the curse worked its way through their life force and he continued to send it further ahead.

He could feel the energy that he absorbed. The more he infected, the stronger he became, and he did everything he could to keep the desire for more at bay.

The crowd dispersed to the sides, pushing at each other to distance themselves from the sudden sickness as those in front of him fell. He kept the area of dark magic moving, those who had been the first infected now dropped to the dirty floor, their faces and skin gone pale from the energy of death. They would recover, their exposure minimum, and without any long-term effects.

In the center the orc and the man were locked hand to hand as they tried to grapple with one another. The one he did not recognize had a pointed blade in his hand and the orc had a slash through the front of his jacket that had a new vibrant pink color that stretched from the opening in small lines that grew longer.

Dark continued his words as he pushed his hands forward. The curse expanded and filled the ground around the two combatants. Greedy claws of ghostly smoke wrapped around both ankles and the power of their hatred came back to him like a full night bender with his own personal keg of ale.

He wanted to cut it off, but the anger in both of them was so great they at first resisted the deathly curse that drained their life force from the ground up. Gritting his teeth he pushed harder, the howls of the demons screamed in his ears, but he bit it back and refused to give.

Floorboards buckled as more of the black magic pushed its way through, decay and death eating away as the two men finally started to weaken.

It started with the grip they each had of the other. The weapon dropped to the ground and once released, Captain Gogron's man took a swing at the one who had cut him. Fist cracked against jaw and they both fell to the ground, their skin gone pale as they hit like rocks thrown from a second story window.

"Everyone stay where you are!" a familiar voice commanded.

Dark pulled back the magic and his body flushed with the grief and pain of the hatred he had absorbed. It hummed in his muscles and the colors of the world rushed back as fast as his heartbeat. His fingers twitched and he could taste the freshly turned soil of the grave.

"What in the bloody seas is going on here?" Coastie Rica demanded.

The big man pushed his way to the front with three more guards at his back. It wasn't much of an effort as those in front barely had the strength to stand, but Dark stepped to the side so that he was not in the way.

Someone must have roused the angry man from his rest. Uniform barely on, he left most of his buttons misaligned, and his pants looked like they had been crumpled up in a corner. Brown stains ran from ankle to knee and the shirt beneath his jacket was open revealing a gold chain that hung from his neck.

"By order of the governor of this city, I hear by arrest anyone and everyone who is still within this establishment within the next five minutes. That is to start with those two."

Rica pointed at the two fighters who struggled to lift their heads off the floor. Men and women did everything they could to not trample each other as they pressed for the door. The other guards, hands on their edged weapons funneled everyone in as orderly a line as they could enforce, the wave of bodies thick and slow moving. They would probably need more than five minutes.

"Good to see you, Rica."

The Coastie glanced at him, his scowl tattooed to his face, and then back down at the two fallen men.

"Why am I not surprised you had your part in this?"

"Only doing the job you paid me for."

"Starting fights in the local taverns?"

Dark put his hands in his pocket, the need for a good cigar overpowering as the magic that still ran through his bones twitched with the need to get out.

"Following leads. Which, by the way, you have one of them sitting there on the floor," Dark said nodding at the fallen human sailor he did not know. "I need a few words with that one. He may know something that will help me get to the bottom of this."

Rica finally turned and looked at him.

"You sure about that?"

Dark nodded.

"First thing in the morning report to lockup. We'll have both of them in there. I'll let their captains come and claim them, but this one I'll hold until you are done. Don't make me push too far."

Dark reached over and took the man's hand in a firm shake. The life force itching to be pulled out.

"I'll be there at first light."

***

"You actually think you'll be able to get him to talk?" Hemley asked.

They walked down Court Street, the first inches of grey appearing on the horizon. The taste of salt was thick in the air, the moving tide keeping the water high this morning. The sound of the seagulls spreading their anger made its way even this far into the city.

"One way or the other he will," Dark answered.

He still wore the same clothes from last night, though the exhaustion had finally hit him. No sleep was available with the amount of power coursing its way through his veins. He paced his room instead. Smoking half a dozen cigars, he played through everything in his head, especially the magic needed to create zombie fish.

Why?

It was a serious commitment and a lot of work to scare off a ship full of orcs because they are particularly good fisherman.

Then why do all of this?

He was no closer now that the sun had broken the horizon than he was in the dead of the night. Hemley on the other hand looked like she had gotten a great night of sleep. Her eyes were bright with her flawless skin as impeccable as ever. Sometimes he wondered if she bathed in the fountain of youth itself as there wasn't a hair out of place in the ponytail she had tied over her shoulder.

"Well, if we run into Captain Gogron, we can ask him a few questions as well. I discovered a few peculiar things while talking to some of the businesses we know around the marina."

"Did you now?"

She smiled at him but said nothing. They approached the city jailhouse where lanterns hung on each side of the single front door. A man in a marina guard's uniform stood out front, his back stiff and eyes forward as he watched their approach. Dark blue pants with an impeccable pressed crease and white shirt with grey overcoat, he was the spitting image of what Rica had been looking to recruit. Dark guessed he probably hadn't been with the department for very long.

"We are here to see Coastie Rica," he said.

The man looked both of them over. There wasn't enough energy left in him to smile, but Hemley did a good job with her presentation. The curtsy earned her a second quick examination from the man.

"Been a busy night. He's a bit occupied at the moment," the guard answered.

Dark didn't have the time or patience for this.

"We are here at the request of Rica himself. If you would go and get him, we'll get this all solved quickly."

The man's eyes narrowed as if he needed a second look.

"As I said," he started.

"Let them in, Leons," Rica called from behind the closed door.

A moment later the entrance to the jail opened and the one they had come to see stood waiting.

"Here at first light, as requested," Dark said.

Rica grunted then tipped his head as if he was wearing a hat to Hemley.

"Never figured you'd be the one to disappoint me. Come in. We have to be quick about it."

With a wave he led them both in. The hall was cramped where boxes lined both walls. Paintings of men and women in uniform peppered the path and the smell of mold and dust was thick enough to force a sneeze out of both him and Hemley.

"Been busy I see," Dark said.

Hemley was too distracted checking out every painting they passed.

"Always am, even if people like you have found it a bit slow. There is always someone doing something they aren't supposed to. I wish they'd give us better quarters though."

They turned and headed down a set of stairs that led below the ground. The air felt noticeably cooler, and the dust gave way to the stench of sweat and urine.

"Already got word from the captains of both these men. Seems like even sailors don't get much sleep. They both want them out before the merchants open shop so they can be back out on the water."

"You take your orders from boat captains now?" Dark asked.

They stepped into a room that had to take up half the building. Five holding cells lined the perimeter walls, three currently empty and two occupied with the men they had been looking for. The two sailors stared at one another, the only thing keeping them from going at each other was the iron bars and the width of the room.

"Fines have been paid. Neither one is demanding payment for damages from the other. Not much I can do. They are yours for the next hour. After that I have to let them go."

"That will do great, Coastie Rica," Hemley chimed in.

She placed a hand on the man's shoulder and he smiled as he went to leave.

"Rica," Dark stopped him. "Any chance you have another room for this one?"

He pointed a thumb over his shoulder at Captain Gogron's man. The coastie looked at both and then nodded. Within a few moments he led the sailor out of the room and closed the door behind him.

Hemley positioned herself against it as she picked at something beneath one of her nails. Dark grabbed a chair from inside one of the cells, dragged it across the floor with all the scratching it would do, and then placed it in front of the remaining man's cell.

"So, it seems you aren't a fan of the sailors from Shallow Isles," he started.

The man spit at him.

"Go piss off. I have no reason to talk to you."

Dark looked over at Hemley.

"You are probably right. Your captain gets here in an hour. Keep your mouth shut, then back on your ship you go. Seems like you have it all figured out."

Dark nodded to Hemley who winked at him.

"Sounds like you might not be as dumb as you look. How about you take a hike and let me enjoy some quiet time with this pretty lady before I sail out. It's rough being out on the water for so long without the feel of a woman for months."

Dark shook his head nice and slow.

"One hour. Not a lot of time for me to get the answers I need," he started, ignoring the comment.

The magic from the night still hissed and spat in the back of his mind, his bones aching for more as he let the magic swirl between his fingers. Within his ears he could hear the voices calling for the pain, wanting so much to devour the life that sat in the room with him.

"But an hour can also feel like a lifetime if I want it to," he finished.

The sailor looked over at him, a smug look on his face.

"You won't touch me. My captain is one of the richest men in this city. He owns half the ships and more than two thirds of the routes. If you lay a hand on me," the sailor bragged.

Everything in the room fell dark and slowly returned to grey as Dark squeezed the magic within his grasp and let it seep out, searching as it slid between the bars. He watched the dark hands and necrotic gas creep its way until it found the man's leg, the demons within so excited it took everything he had not to allow it to push up like a spear to the chest.

The man gasped as it took hold.

With a twist of his wrist, he felt the man's heart flutter, the strength he had of his own convictions draining away and filling the gap Dark always felt within his chest. Scratching at his throat, the sailor struggled to breathe as the dark curse made its way up his body. A thousand hands poked and prodded their way around, tiny bits finding finger holds within scratches and old scars, the death pulling itself inside at every chance it got.

"See, I control if you live or die within that cell. Not Rica. Not Hemley. I hold the key. You can talk with me like a gentleman over the next hour, or I can make sure every last minute of your miserable life feels like this. Then, when I'm done with you, they'll find you sleeping on your bed. You do look a little tired. Do you feel tired?"

The sailor's eyes were wide with fear, the muscles in his neck stretched as if he was drowning in invisible water. With a flick of his wrist, Dark called the magic back. The man almost collapsed from the pain.

"Do we have a deal? Or will your captain find you sleeping in your bed never to wake up? A victim to unfortunate circumstances."

"He'll, he'll blame that orc friend of yours."

Dark shook his head.

"You mean the one I purposely made sure wasn't in the room? A dozen witnesses will speak to the fact that he was locked up on the other side of the building."

What little color was left in the man's complexion drained as he looked to Hemley. She did not move, her attention more on whatever it was that she was trying to dig out from beneath one of her nails.

"Please…please, I don't know anything. I swear."

Dark leaned back in his chair, his arms crossed, and one finger twirling with a small amount of magic working its way from the tip.

"Lying isn't a good way to start. I heard you back at the bar. You know about the problems the men from the Shallow Isles have been having with their catches. No one but the authorities and those on the ship know. How did you find out? Who told you?"

The sailor's eyes widened and flicked back and forth. He licked his dry lips and then he stopped where his eyes could follow the twirling finger.

"Please…I heard it on board. People have been talking about it for weeks. It isn't…it isn't what you think."

Dark leaned forward, his eyes narrowing.

"What isn't how I think it is? You aren't giving me anything to work with here and I'm losing my patience."

The man scooted himself as far back in the cell as he could, his hands gripping the cloth that covered his steel grated bed.

"No one is doing anything to the Orcs, I swear. If it was one of us, my captain would know. We own too many of the ships. It's the rumors. The rumors that make it to us."

"What are the rumors? You've got yourself one chance to tell me the truth."

Dark let the magic at his fingertips create a dark circle that floated in the air for a moment before dissipating like smoke.

"They are doing it to themselves. Their death magic. They bring it upon themselves. Legend has it that the Shallow Isles is where the death magic comes from. Its source is in that vile place. Whatever is happening to them, they are doing it to themselves."

"Ah bugger off," Dark spat.

He threw his chair across the room where it hit another cell and came to a stop. With a wave of his hand, Hemley opened the door and led them both out.

"Not what you wanted?" she asked.

He grit his teeth.

"The man isn't lying. He is little more than a drunk bastard, but he's telling the truth. At least what he knows as the truth."

"How can you tell?"

Hemley put her hand on his shoulder and they both stopped before they reached the front of the jail. There was no one around, not even any site of Captain Gogron's man or Rica himself.

"The rumors. He's at least half correct."

"Which part?"

Dark shook his head and closed his eyes. Memories that he wished had stayed buried rose to the surface like an old ghost ship coming to haunt him until the end of his days.

"The death magic. Whatever is killing and bringing these fish back, it originates out in those Isles."

"Gogron never mentioned that before."

"Probably because if it really got out that they were transporting those who practiced these arts to the mainland, they'd never be allowed in port. The man has no idea I could possibly already know."

Hemley stiffened he shoulders and looked down the hall that would bring them back out onto the street.

"Seems like we'll have to go find the captain and ask him a few questions ourselves."

***

The men were busy.

Shouts moved where the bodies wouldn't fit as cargo and empty netting was carried onto waiting vessels. The entire marina was filled with merchants, sailors, hands-for-hire, and city guards. There was hardly anywhere to move and going someplace with determination didn't help.

To their amazement, space finally opened up as they got closer to the ship they knew so well.

Night's Mistress.

The early morning carried with it crisp cool air and the freshness of it helped Dark push back the pulses that bounced within him. The magic wanted out. It needed to be released, but the cool autumn morning was a good way to keep it at bay.

Something about the light.

Mystery and rumors always talked about necromancy and its dark ways, but even the most uneducated myth at times is buried in a dusting of truth. His magic worked best at night. Sometimes even too well, but it wasn't like he was left undefended during the day. It just wasn't as capable as it was when he could wrap himself in the warm blanket of the shadows.

His knuckles popped as he clenched his fists. The flicker of power that burned at his fingertips was there if he needed it. Probably him overthinking everything. There were too many people here to start a problem. A riot, or at least the mayhem the city guard would create would be too much. It could ruin a captain's business no matter how rich he was.

Pushing their way through the last few lines of bodies, the pier that led up to Captain Gogron's ship was full of life, but not nearly as much as those crowded around the other ships. There were those who found Orcs not to their liking, but this example of distancing was a bit to the extreme. Empty nets and broken crates were lined along the edge of the water and the men took little effort to load them.

Maybe the sailor wasn't lying about the word getting out. It was time to see if he was lying about the other part as well.

"Captain Gogron!" Dark yelled.

Many of the men stopped what they were doing. Some held crates over their shoulders like they weighed little more than a bundle of sticks. Others pulled rope, large circles of it wrapped around muscle corded arms and shoulders, knuckles turned white as their hands gripped the line like iron. No one moved. No one spoke. More than a dozen eyes waited.

"Captain," he tried again.

"Maybe he isn't here," Hemley whispered.

She tucked herself in beside his shoulder, her weight almost insignificant, but her stance put her slightly ahead of him.

"He's here," Dark said. "See, his man from last night is right up there on the ship. He wouldn't be out if Gogron didn't come and get him personally."

A few moments passed before the orcs turned back to their duties. The show was over. Nothing to see here.

Gritting his teeth, Dark moved up the pier. He was going to get his answers. One way or the other.

The sailors didn't move out of his way as he pushed forward. Hundreds of pounds of muscles, it jostled him back and forth to force his way up to the plank that would get him onto the deck. Hemley stayed right on his heels. He could feel her more than see her as they rose above the water and made their way aboard ship.

"Captain! I want to see the captain!"

The men on board did little more than those on the pier. They stopped their duties and stared, all of them silent until the one he had found fighting in the bar stepped to the side until he made his way beside the cabin and disappeared within.

"Looks like we get to speak with the captain after all."

Hemley stood beside him, her eyes searching, and he let his magic pulse a little more through his veins, the dampening he usually practiced held back for now.

"Ah, Detective, for what matter do I owe the pleasure of speaking with you today," Gogron said as he exited the cabin.

Dressed in his usual uniform pants, he wore no shirt, his green skin vibrant in the morning light, white scars decorating his skin as he crossed the deck.

"The lady, Hemley, how it is great to see you this morning."

With a gentle touch, the captain lifted her hand up and placed a small kiss across her knuckles with a thousand gold coin smile on his face.

"Your man there is lucky he isn't chained in a cage right now," Dark started.

Gogron looked back where the sailor waited silently.

"I've been told I have you to thank for that. Seems like it was a bit of your personal magic that stopped the incident from becoming, how should I say it, messy."

Dark looked over at the sailor who had a look on his face somewhere between mild irritation and pure anger.

"Not such a smart idea to be out drinking and getting in fights in a city I hear you aren't as popular as I was led to believe."

The big captain crossed his arms, scars twisting and muscles bulging as he did so.

"My people aren't always welcome no matter where we go. Some say it is our customs, others the color of our skin. Would you venture to take a guess which it is, Detective?"

Dark could feel the tension in the air around him, almost more than he could taste the decay that boiled around his fingertips.

"Could it be possible that wherever you happen to do business a plague follows that decimates fellow sailors until you are the only one that remains?" Hemley asked as she stepped forward.

Her shoulders were back, fists clenched, but the big orc still towered over her.

"Those are big accusations from a detective's assistant."

Not liking those words, Dark took a step

forward, his hand opening, the darkness of the world growing a shade closer.

"Are you threatening us, Captain?"

Gogron's smile returned.

"No, no my friend. I know you and lady Hemley are only trying to complete your mission. I apologize if I came off too strong. It was an early morning, even for me. The men grow weary of recent events, and many look forward to the venture home. Especially those I spoke of when we last met who still haven't grown their sea legs yet. Family and friends are greatly missed."

Dark looked over at Hemley, her eyes still little balls of fire as she stared at the big captain.

"So, you are returning home? The unfortunate events here forgotten?"

Gogron shook his head, the tension across his chest softening.

"It pains me to say, I do not have another choice. The coin grows thin. I allowed the men a night of relaxing for the hard work done, replenished our stores for the voyage, but little remains in the coffers. I can get us back home, but then there will be long discussions on the viability of our business in waters that do not belong to us."

He could feel the tension in Hemley dissipate as he stepped in front of her, his own magic pulling back into his veins. The demons inside his head quieted, but the pain they inflicted still cracked at the inside of his skull.

"Maybe we can still be of some help, Captain. How about we go out for one more catch? Tell your men that if they can hold it together for one more voyage, I'll see if I can help turn your fortunes around."

One eyebrow shifted on the big orc's face. He did not answer at first, a quick glance at the men that moved along his boat.

"I am not sure there is anything you can do, Detective, unless you can bring the catch back to life. But, out of respect for what you are attempting to do, I can grant you one more trip. It will have to be a short one though, because supplies do not come cheap."

Dark glanced across the marina. Men and women worked like ants as they crawled over rigging and scurried up the ropes. Everyone was rushing to follow the tide out to sea, he hoped that the fishermen wouldn't be the only ones.

***

His stomach churned and all he could taste was the smoke of his last cigar and the coffee he had forced down when the sun had broken the horizon in the morning. He gripped the railing of the boat and the world spun before his eyes, but he did his best to push it all back. Hemley stood at his side, the wind that pushed off the sea whipping her hair over her shoulder, and he could not help the mixed feelings about the smile that spread across her face. Anger or enjoyment? It was nice having her there, but why did she have to be happy all the time.

"I hope you have a plan," she whispered over the wind.

There was no one within earshot of where they stood. Gogron's men were busy at work either pulling lines, working the mast, or doing any of several various tasks he had assigned them. The word was given very firmly that they were not to be disturbed at any point during this trip.

"I have what I have," he answered.

A devious smile formed across her lips.

"You have nothing, do you? We are out on a ship in the middle of the sea, and you have no idea what we are doing. Sometimes you surprise me, Shadow-walker."

Her hands moved in waves through the passing breeze. She never asked him to explain himself. It would take nothing for him to head into this without a single idea if it would work, yet she'd still be here with him.

In his gut a sharp pinch reminded him that he wasn't sure if he was willing to live with that.

"We are closing in on the fishing grounds," Captain Gogron called from the door to the cabins.

Dark watched as the orc took his big strides that carried him across the ship. The confidence and the unbridled energy the man had carried when they first met were replaced with an exhaustion that hung heavy from his shoulders. The life that had pulsed from him drained and a half-empty husk was left in its wake.

"I can smell it already," Dark said in return.

To which he was not lying. Decay filled the air and the debris from earlier ships remained scattered, though somehow he doubted they had fully reached their destination. Something about this trip made it feel shorter, as if the disease and poison was making its way toward the shore and they didn't need to cross such a great distance to find it.

"Will you need us to drop a line when we get there?" the big captain asked.

Dark turned back toward the marina they had left hours earlier. They were alone out here on the sea. A single ship floating within the decaying remains of a magic that brought the dead back to life.

"Yes, Captain, but drop anchor if you can immediately after. I don't want us going anywhere anytime soon."

Both Hemley and Gogron stared at him.

Dropping anchor in the middle of the sea was a risk enough. In an area full of necrotic dead coming from an unknown source was something else entirely.

"You are absolutely sure about this?" Hemley asked.

He nodded and then turned back out to sea. They were still alone, and the sun was high. There was only going to be a single shot at this. Either he was correct, and they'd stop this here and now, or he'd made a fatal error and he'd be lucky if Gogron didn't continue on to the Shallow Isles and drag Hemley back with them after tossing him into the sea with the zombie fish.

"All right men, drop a net! We are fishing!" Captain Gogron yelled.

The men stared at their captain. No one moved, many turning their eyes to where Hemley and himself stood.

"What are you all waiting for? Get to your posts!"

As if smacked in the face with a fist from the big orc, the men jumped to their duties. Reaching for the railing of the deck, Dark closed his eyes and took in a deep breath. He could feel the necrotic energy making its way off the sea's surface and onto the boat.

"You, OK?" Hemley asked.

He kept his eyes shut, nodded, and put finger up to his lips.

Slowly he let his own magic seep out from his fingers where it ran down the railing, over the edge of the boat, and down the hull into the water. There was so much there. It swirled for leagues. Dark, putrid poison that was unchecked and spreading as fast as the waves could carry it.

It was also hungry.

Quietly, he let the sounds of the nets splashing into the water and the men who worked them roll over him. He followed his senses deeper. There was a pulsing that pulled at them. A heartbeat that was speeding up. As if….

Dark's eyes popped open.

"Captain!" he tried to yell, but it was too late.

A crack of thunder broke the open silence of the sea and all color drained from the sunny day. The world dropped into that space between life and death as Hemley and the men of the ship finally felt what it was like to be him. Poisoned water boiled beside them. Geysers erupted into the air as a black oily tentacle, almost the size of the ship, broke free and swept for those who stood on the deck.

"Down!" Dark screamed.

He grabbed Hemley by the arm and threw her and himself down onto the wooden planks, the unforgiving surface sending painful spasms through his body. Many of the men did the same, the orc trapped on top of the mast unfortunate to get caught in the large swipe screamed as he was hurled into the rolling waves, his voice never returning.

"To arms men!" Captain Gogron ordered.

Several of the sailors grabbed pikes and spears from compartments hidden within the deck before they ran for the railing closest to the emerging monster.

"What is that?" Hemley screamed.

Dark looked at her. Her eyes were wide and for once there was fear he had never seen before. Out on the water another large tentacle covered in suckers and dripping oily sludge reared back for a swing of its own before it was met with half a dozen spears that split flesh and pierced deep into the muscle beneath.

A scream from the depths of the seven hells itself erupted from the water. Black sludge erupted high into the sky.

"I'm not sure. Whatever it is, it wasn't here the first time," Dark answered.

Pushing himself to his feet, he grabbed her hand and pulled her up.

"We need to help them," she said.

They watched for a moment as men grabbed more spears and two had crossbows that twanged as they fired arrows.

"I fully intend to," he said in return.

Pulling her along, they headed for the cabins, the sound of men screaming and the splashing of water passing them by.

"But the monster is," she started until he kicked a door at the rear of the cabin open.

One of the orcs from inside of the ship stood inside, his eyes wide and reddened, a dagger with blood dripping already in his hand.

"You had to," he started, but never finished.

Hemley, his grip on her hand gone, was through the door before he could stop her. The orc's blade came up, but only half an arm's length before her fist crunched into his throat, the sound of the cracking evident even from where he was standing.

Clutching at the damage, the man stumbled a few steps back before falling against a back wall, his green face reddening and swelling as he struggled to breathe.

"How did you?" Dark asked.

Hemley glared at him, her hands balled, and the smile he had grown to know now a distant memory.

"Not now, Shadow-walker. These men need help."

The remaining words froze on his lips. Another orc, muscles bunched and eyes breathing fire, exited from the doorway that opened to the ladder that led below. Hemley spun, her hand shooting forward.

Staggering, the orc caught himself on the doorway with one big arm, his other hand reaching for his neck. A flash of silver sparkled before drowning in dark blood, the dagger in his throat piercing through the flesh. A kick to his chest broke his lock on the frame and he fell down the opening, his body hitting the lower deck with a loud thud.

"Stay behind me," Hemley ordered.

Dark had nothing to say. He stared at the dead man on the floor at his feet, eyes wide and glassed over, cheeks swollen and blue.

"You don't need tell me twice."

She turned back to the ladder, glanced down, and with the elegance of a leaf in the wind, she slid down the railing. He was not as elegant. Taking the rungs two at a time. Hemley waited at the bottom, daggers in each hand.

From down below he could still hear the battle above, but now there were words that whispered in the shadows. Incantations from a lost age. The blood in his veins boiled as the magic tickled his senses. The shadows in the corners grew and he watched as the world around him turned a darker grey.

He closed his eyes and allowed the necromancy to flow into him. His muscles tensed and his body drew in the cold. Opening his eyes, Hemley flowed like the sun in the darkened world, the daggers in her hands bright stars as she stalked forward.

His step behind hers, they moved deeper into the ship. Closed doors lined the swaying hall, the smoke of necrotic magic leaching from below the barred barriers.

In front of them the magic grew as thick as a fog along the floor. The attack on his senses grew stronger. His feet dragged down with dark mud. Hemley seemed less affected, her strides confident, her head swiveling as they watched for attacks from the edges.

Their world turned upside down as the ship rocked to the side, throwing them against the wall. Pain rocked his body as they both bounced back and forward as the ship shifted, the floor catching both of them.

"We need to hurry!" he yelled.

Hemley turned to him from where she had fallen. Eyes narrowed and intense, she nodded and climbed back to her feet with the grace of a dancer. His joints popped and ached as he struggled, the magic trying to pull him to the depths through the boards and into the ocean below.

"How much further?" Hemley asked.

They were getting close, the screams of demons wailing in his ears.

"As far back as we can go."

She turned and continued on. He struggled, but stayed as close as he could.

Without warning the nearest door to their left shattered and a mass of muscle and bone slammed into Hemley. With a scream they hit the wall, the planks buckling. Hands up, he didn't hold back.

Black light oozed from his fingers, wrapped around the orc and ripped the man from her. She wilted to the ground as the attacker was lifted in the air. Dark could feel the life force within him start to drain and he pushed it further. Spreading his hands, he watched as the man's arms and legs spread, his body suspended. With a snap of his fingers and a spread of his arms the body exploded into a gory mess, the whole of his life force slamming into him at full speed.

He staggered, the euphoria swimming its way through his veins and into his brain. Darkness erupted through his vision, the need for more overwhelming him. Blood filled his mouth, but he bit down and forced it away. They would not survive if he lost control. Grabbing Hemley's hand he pulled her back to her feet.

"You, OK?" he asked.

Blood trickled from the corner of her mouth, but she grinned back at him and stepped forward to take the lead once again.

Each new door they approached with caution. Hemley's eyes scanned every inch they covered. Once again, the ship listed, this time Hemley stayed on her feet, but he did his best not to bounce too much against the wall.

"Last door straight ahead," she said.

The grip on her daggers tightened as her knuckles whitened. Letting the magic build up, he could feel the pressure in his chest push against his bones, ready to explode.

"Out of my way," he said in return.

Hemley stepped out of the way, and he unleashed a fraction of what he held back.

Wood splintered as the entrance erupted. Daggers up, Hemley jumped in, a hand flashing as the blade flew at someone in the back. Dark let the magic swirl around his fingers as he followed her in, his vision pushing through the darkness.

"You are too late," a voice called out from the chaos.

Dark through up his hands, his magic forming a wall in front of him as the attack landed with so much force it buckled his knees.

A body laid across a makeshift table of lined chairs in the center of the room. The sailor from the tavern fight. Blood drained from arms and legs, chalices catching life's fluid at each corner. Over the sacrifice, an orc he had not seen before held its arms high, fingers twirling. Dark veins spread from his eyes, the magic spreading across its skin.

Unable to hesitate, Dark unleashed a torrent of his own magic, the evil void swirling through the air.

Smoke rippled in a wall in front of the man, the magic blocked before hitting its target.

"Do you really think you can fight me? When I grind your bones to dust, we will return to the Shallow Isles where we belong. The world of man is an abomination on this world. We do not need your poison spreading to our homes."

With a flick of his hand a rush of necrotic hands formed and rushed across the room, Dark was forced to roll to the side, his beaten body aching. His strength wavered as he climbed back to his knees.

"You are killing your own kind!"

The orc smiled.

"Sacrifices will be made. Those who think our world should mix with the taint of yours will learn."

More magic shot across the room and it took everything Dark had to throw up a wall to deflect the power. Pain reverberated through his bones, the depths of Hell calling his name through the voices in his head.

Every muscle in his body cramped as he forced himself to his feet, the world swirling.

"I will stop you," Dark said, his voice wavering.

A smile spread across the man's face.

Fingers twirling, dark snakes wove themselves between his fingers, the shadows pulling to him. Dark could feel the shivers running through his body, the depths this man was pulling from reached further than he had ever even thought of reaching for.

His own magic struggled to form, the energy and force needed draining into the well the sorcerer was pulling from. Gritting his teeth, he reached for everything he could muster, anything that would fight back against the incoming onslaught.

Silver flashed in the darkness and slammed into the wall of magic behind the man. Nothing pierced, but the rippling was evident and deep. Dark turned and there stood Hemley, one hand empty, dagger in the other.

"I will handle you after," the sorcerer said.

One hand shot out and the magic that slammed into Hemley sent her spinning into the corner of the cabin.

Dark did not hesitate. His magic flared and he sent it spiraling through the space between them. The man's magic pivoted and formed a wall between them, but with a flick of his fingers Dark pulled it down before it struck. Down into the floor it sank, the boards opening and allowing it to sink into the depths.

The sorcerer spun, his hand coming forward and the snakes of death shooting out.

Dark let himself drop to the floor, his back hitting the wall as another flash of silver spun across the room. The sorcerer screamed and staggered. Reaching as deep as he could, Dark pulled from the depths his magic had reached and the boards to the ship cracked. Hands grabbed at the orc's ankles, the magic sinking in deep.

Inside he could feel the lifeforce pull into him like hot metal as it burned down to his soul. Everything blackened, his eyes watered, but he bit down and squeezed harder. The sorcerer pushed against him, but Dark fought with everything he had.

"Is that all you have?" the man said, his voice echoing but a small waver leaked into the words.

Hands lifting, dark blood swirled from the chalices that remained at the four corners of the corpse. A disk of rippling blood floated above the floor; a small spin started as words that did not belong in this world spread from his lips.

Dark bit down harder, pulled his magic as hard as he could and drained as fast as he could. The force at which the life hit him knocked the wind from his lungs and his muscles cramped.

He was spent. This was all he had as the sorcerer continued to build his magic, the disk spinning faster.

"I will pull the life from you as I have this man who gave everything to bring us back home. Your power will speed us in our journey home, so do not think that your sacrifice will be in vain."

Dark took in a deep breath. There was nothing he could do. This was the end.

"Fight back, Shadow-walker," Hemley's voice broke in. "Go where he will not."

He could not see her, but her words were as clear as if she was sitting right beside him.

Pulling his magic back, he let it sink back into the boards of the ship, the hands fighting his call. The need for the sorcerer's life force was so great he almost couldn't do it. It was enticing, luring, and intoxicating. The emptiness inside of him hollowed him out. The dryness in his mouth cracked into blood between his teeth.

He was just too powerful, too strong. There was no matching his abilities. The darkness he had pulled from the dead sailor was too much. Closing his eyes, he let himself drain into the shadows, everything he could give for one more try.

Sinking his teeth into the darkness around him, he let his magic bubble from the sea below. The necrotic energy reaching the depths by which he had never seen. Eyes bleeding, he pulled, reached down to the beast below and yanked for every ounce of life he could.

With his call the ship listed, and the room tilted to its side. Dark tried to hold himself in place, but he slid as the sounds of boards snapping filled the room. Dark water rushed in, the smell of death and decay filling the room. Within moments items began to float, the ship now taking on water.

"What have you done?" the sorcerer demanded.

Dark smiled his own devilish grin.

"If I can't beat you, I'll make sure you never make it home."

All the energy in his body was gone and he could taste the salt water as it washed against his face. White foam swirled from the gap in the hull as more boards splintered and the ship tilted in the opposite direction, throwing them all the opposite way.

There was nothing he could do as Dark fell beneath the coming water. The words of the shadows filled his ears, calling his name, but he could no longer hear the chants of the sorcerer.

A calmness came over his body. At least he had done something good with his death. He closed his eyes.

White light pushed its way through his lids as a firm grip took his shoulder.

"Get up, Shadow-walker," Hemley said.

Dark opened his eyes, and she stood above him, pulling him above the level of the rising sea.

"We need to reach the deck," she yelled.

With strength beyond her frame, she forced him to his feet. The water was already to their waists. A quick look over where the sorcerer once stood revealed nothing but a dark circle that was quickly opening as more water broke its way in.

Cold ice ran up his spine as she dragged him along. Wet clothes, dark magic, and exhaustion weighed him down, but he lifted one foot in front of the other. The whole ship tilted, it slowed them down, but they made slow progress.

"We…we aren't going to make it," he said, the shadows quickly chasing them.

"Keep moving. We'll make it."

The floor tilted again, and the hall became a climb as they tried to outrun the water. Grabbing the walls, they pulled themselves up the climb, water grabbing at their feet.

"You first," Hemley demanded when they reached the ladder.

Dark went to object, but she shoved him forward. The metal rungs were ice cold and his muscles cramped as he reached up and pulled. She put her shoulder beneath him and pushed.

Slowly, hand over hand, he lifted himself. At his feet he could feel Hemley's hands and the encroaching water. His body ached more and more, but he reached the upper deck and fell topside. Hemley toppled after him and fell where she laid on top of him.

"There you two are," Captain Gogron's voice rumbled. "You'll have plenty of time for that later."

Large hands grabbed both of them and lifted them to their feet. The ship continued to shift back and forth as the prow climbed higher, the sound of boards and floors shattering created a thunder of its own as the center of boat broke apart and sank.

"Over the side as fast as you can go!" the big captain shouted.

Pushing them forward they left the cabins and spilled out onto the deck. Men were grabbing anything that would help them float as they jumped over the edge.

"What about?" Dark started.

The captain shoved him forward, but there was no need for an answer. Pieces of ship debris were scattered in the water, a dark oil spread across the surface, but there was no beast. He could now feel the magic that had pulled the beast into this world was missing. The only thing in the air was the taste of salt and the shouts of men as they tried to escape the sinking ship.

"Over you two go," Captain Gogron said.

There was no stopping him as he grabbed both of them by the pants, lifted them up and dropped them over the railing.

The sea rushed to greet them, the salty water quick to fill his mouth. Using all the strength he had, he broke the surface, the cool water coming in as he choked out and struggled to breathe.

"Dark!" Hemley yelled.

She swam toward him, a large piece of debris tucked under her arm.

"Look who showed up," she added.

Following her arm, he looked out away from the sinking ship. Two white masts shined in the afternoon light. Lines were being thrown from the boat as sailors swam their way toward safety. The yachts sailors helping pull those who reached first up onto the deck.

"Seems like our Lady is here to save the day," Hemley said.

Dark let his arms rest for a moment on the piece of broken deck.

"It looks that way," he muttered, his legs slowly kicking.

***

The sea remained calm as the sun fell below the horizon, pieces of the Night's Mistress floating with the waves. Deep red waves streaked across the sky, broken clouds stretching, and sea birds circling high above.

"I'm sorry about your ship," Dark said.

Captain Gogron stepped up beside him, his shoulders bare where Dark kept a warm blanket wrapped around his shoulders. The big captain had borrowed one of the tri-pointed hats from the men of the ship, his bare arms crossed over his ship.

"Nothing more than wood and oil, Detective. There will be others," he said.

Dark kept his eyes out on the water.

"And your men, Gogron. We are sorry for those you have lost," Hemley added.

The big captain nodded.

"Some of them will be missed. Others are lost as they should be."

Dark pulled his blanket tighter and looked at Hemley. She had a similar green blanket around her body, her usually perfect hair twisted into knots from where it had dried.

"Tell me, Detective. How did you know?" Gogron asked.

It was time for Dark to shrug.

"The man who picked a fight with your sailor. He said you were doing this to yourself," he said.

"And the history that follows your business, Captain. People may hate you, but it followed you like a plague," Hemley added. "You seem to be a genuinely good man, Captain. Spending your money to ship men and dead fish everywhere seems to be a rather bad choice to make a successful living."

"Plus, there are people looking to your success. If it was a plague that was a trap for you, there would be no reason to be here, would there be, Lady Alexa," Dark said.

He turned and there she was, her dress a bright reflection in the fading light.

"I would say it was good to see you, Detective, but trouble seems to follow you."

Pulling the blanket off his shoulders, Dark shook it out before wrapping it to add a second layer onto Hemley.

"It is what I get paid to do. But I should leave you with the Captain here, I assume you have a lot to talk about."

"Speaking of trouble, I hear you have some dealings with a certain Mr. Braco."

Dark stopped, held his lips shut, and waited. The breeze from the water could barely push away the silence.

"Very well, Detective. I respect a man who keeps his business to himself when the time is right, but Mr. Braco is an acquaintance of mine."

This time Hemley stepped forward and positioned herself slightly in front of him. Lady Alexa folded her hands in front of herself.

"I've spoken with Mr. Braco. For your service here, all business debts you have with the man are forgiven. You shall not hear from him again, or he may risk the profits of our business together."

Dark went to say something but stopped. Captain Gogron remained silent with his customary smile, and Hemley let herself slide back behind his shoulder.

Lady Alexa only nodded.

"Hemley, how about you and I find a place to relax in the cabin. It is going to be awhile before we make it back to the marina."

Arm tucked into his elbow, he led her to the cabins of the ship, the rocking of the waves no longer upsetting his stomach.

The End

Without the Ticket

By
William J. Seymour
© 2017

The Circus has arrived. Everyone in the city is going. Everyone but Levi. A boy, raised on the streets does not have the money or the means to pay for a ticket. If he is going to get a chance to see the show, he must find another way in. One that won't cost him his head.

It's almost noon, they'll start any minute!

Levi dashed down the cobblestone street, dust kicking into the air from the heels of his tattered sandals and frayed cloth pants as he rounded the corners of market tables with piles of imported fruits and metal and clay works for sale. He dashed beneath the stares of street urchins keeping one eye on their wares and the other on the street boy as he waded his way through the tide of cloth and heat, the salty smell of deep summer heavy in the dry air. The noble's looked down their noses as he struggled to move through the sea of bodies, their brightly colored silks of red and purple a contrast to the grays of stone that climbed high upon the castle walls that stood to their north, overlooking the land with an ever-watchful eye.

He knew their look. Their noses turned up, their lips curved into a snarl, and the glare of their eyes, looking at the dirt on his skin as if it was a disease. It was as if the earth at their feet wouldn't stick to them if they rolled around in it, somehow graced by the gods themselves, they were immune to the muck that collected at their feet. Levi knew this wasn't so, he'd seen it himself. Just this spring he'd watched from behind a set of barrels, hoping to find one with a loose top that would net him a small dinner, if not a fortune in fresh fish dragged in from the river Orlean. Looking through the crack between them, his narrow shoulders and frail frame hid easily in the shadows of the afternoon sun as the snow-white carriage had wheeled itself through the streets, its tires bouncing over the loose stones and splashing the spring rains as the horses pulled their load.

He had heard it was a princess from the Kingdom of Lyconia, promised in marriage to the King himself, but none of that had seemed correct. Levi wasn't as smart as some of the other street boys, having grown up since the age of five on handouts and whatever he could steal, but he knew if it were a princess, she wouldn't have had to sneak into the city on a late spring afternoon. There would be a royal entourage, guards in gilded armor accompanying her till the King could take her hand and help her step from the carriage himself in his first appearance before the people in years.

No, this was different. Well-built and dressed in the finest wood, the expensive cart was too simple for a princess from one of the finest kingdom's in Pangeria, but it was also alone. One door, four horses and a single man out front with a wide brim hat and a long beard that hung gray and down below his legs. The King himself didn't arrive to let her out, nor did they open the gates. Instead, a door guard, dressed in dull chainmail that ended at his knees, leather boots tied loosely up his calf, and steel spear leaning against the stone palisade that extended a hundred feet above their heads. A helmet which he left by his station sat collecting dust, the sweat rim around his head where his dark ear length hair pasted to his skin evidence of his discomfort. A conversation passed between the soldier and the driver before he moved to open the side exit.

Levi had watched as she had stepped out, dressed in silks down to her ivory slippers. His breath was stolen as she emerged from the darkened interior, a shining star in the afternoon already lit by a high sun and clouds that had broken apart hours before. Without making a sound, she stepped down the small ladder that was built beneath the door and smiled as she came to rest near the guard, who by comparison was not pleased judging from the frown that he carried. Her skin was nearly as illuminated as her dress, pale and clear, yet young and vibrant as it stood in stark contrast to the fire-red hair that fell loosely to the small of her back. There wasn't a tangle or knot in the strands that flowed in the soft breeze, moving like it was blessed by the angels from above, she was a beauty lost in a sea of sun-bleached stone and drying water.

Curiosity had almost gotten Levi that day, wanting to move closer to see who the unannounced guest of the palace was until one of the front horses became spooked and tried to bolt forward. Mud and dark water splashed into the air as the rear of the wagon turned and slapped into the fair lady and left her splayed across the cobblestone and the guard swearing at the old man and the four beasts he now struggled to control.

Fear and amusement fought within him as he bit his lip, stifling the laugh that almost leaked out at the sight, horses neighing and the guard swearing up a storm that would make a priest bless himself to save himself from going to hell just for hearing the words used. Then to Levi's astonishment, she had joined in. The language used burned into the afternoon air as the guard's face reddened to match the color of her cheeks. Black mud and Levi guessed more than likely droppings from the horses themselves, covered the young lady from chest to foot. Grease ran down the fine silks in droplets and rivers as she stomped her slipper covered foot into a puddle and sent more up her legs.

She cursed and demanded attention, but there was no one in sight, save the guard, and the older driver, who sat back with the reins laid softly on his lap and chewing a piece of straw between his lips like a cow.

"I will not see the King like this!"

The words flew out like daggers, but the guard only shrugged.

"Ya can see him naked if you like," the guard said.

Levi could see the smallest evidence of a smile on his face now.

"He will hear about this!"

She stamped her foot into the puddle again, and this time Levi noticed she was no longer standing level. She favored her left as if it was shorter than the other.

"You see that he does. Haven't seen the man in years."

The woman crossed her arms over her breasts and let out an angry sigh that Levi could hear across the street. He watched as her beautiful hair clumped and left streaks of brown and black across the back of her dress.

"Will you at least see me in through the front gate?"

With a nod, the guard turned back to where his helmet sat and the small wood door that was dwarfed by the portcullis that reached the top of the wall above.

Metal rang into the air as the steel helmet hit solid oak in two quick successions.

"Open the door, you mule-brained idiots. Don't you see we have a lady here?"

Hinges creaked as the entrance opened to the shadows within. Levi watched as the woman wiped her dress a few more times before stepping forward. There would be no removing all the mud and filth that had ruined that dress. In astonishment, Levi was barely able to catch the one thing that both the guard and even the woman had seemed to miss. Her left foot. She was no longer wearing the ivory slipper. Mud and muck had clung to her skin as she stepped within the castle walls, her slipper now missing.

Darting around the barrels, Levi ran to where she had been standing, her cart now rumbling in the distance as it made its way along the wall. The front sentry was still in the doorway, watching her disappear within as Levi examined the murky water of the street. Brown and rusty, the pool had a film on it that glowed an almost green as he reached down inside, the liquid cold against his warm skin.

Soft yet sturdy, he pulled the shoe from the watery grave. Wet grit and chunks floated within as small streams flowed from the side and splashed at his feet. The slipper was not big, barely longer than his hand. How young was she? Barely larger than a child's foot surely.

"Hey, what are you doing there you rat?" the guard's voice growled.

Levi didn't look up, the man's shadow already towering next to him and the ominously pointed edge of his sword longer than his leg wavering too close to his own shadow. Using the wings of a frightened child, Levi bolted down the street and turned down the first darkened corner he could find. He didn't hear the sounds of pursuit as he hid in the shadows, one hand firmly against the stone wall and the other wrapped around the slipper, its rubber sole stiff yet the stained cloth above soft within his grip.

Who was she?

He didn't wait to find out, he had a story to tell.

* * *

The red tarp extended higher than the nearest building, the flag atop its pointed peak whipping in the wind, its orange, blue and green rolling as the colors waved in a rippling dance. Levi could hear the voices of hundreds of people, if not thousands shouting and whispering, a mosaic of excitement and wonder, curiosity and amazement, as he moved with the mass of citizens, the flow of the crowded slowly wading its way toward the marked entrance of the tent.

Marco the Magnificent and His Family of Famous Oddities

The news had been all over the city since the beginning of summer, from rumors spread by traveling merchants and farmers pulling wagons from nearby villages to the signs that had appeared overnight like magic two weeks ago. Tacked to walls and stone, questions painted in red, and drawings of unknown creatures spread throughout the land.

It has four paws, and claws as large as your hand. It will devour you in one sitting yet will stop and play with a simple ball in the sand. Are you ready for the real King of the Jungle?

Has your hairy uncle gone missing? Does your aunt seem to climb on your nerves and enjoy her fair share of tropical fruit? Don't worry, they will soon return home like you've never seen them before!

The circus was coming to the kingdom for the first time that Levi could remember. There were whispers of bears and lions as never seen before. Men with multiple heads and women strong enough to break down stone walls with their bare hands. All the stories that dreams were made of and Levi didn't want to miss a minute of it.

He could feel rough hands push him forward as the crowd made its way toward the entrance. Nobles and peasants alike rushed along as the city tried to file underneath the red tarp, its color as deep and dark as blood, yet everyone smiled just being around it. Ripples like waves on a sea of dry air filtered through, the thunderous bellowing of the cloth giving the simple structure an otherworldly feeling. High above, the sun burned like a fiery orb as the midday spectacle would soon begin.

Roars and other sounds that Levi could not recognize called out from within the canopy, animals that both stopped Levi's heart and caused it to rush faster. What was in there? Where had Marco gotten them all? He bet the man had seen all the corners of the world, now traveling along the five nations, he must have been showing kings and queens all that stood just outside their borders.

"I've heard they have men so tiny that they can fit a small legion inside a single cart."

"Well, I've heard they have creatures as large as the castle wall with ears that can hear for miles. They say they can also walk on logs and dance better than your husband!"

Levi could hear strangers speak and laugh as he slipped between legs and around dresses, the people of the city just as excited as he was. He was getting closer now, the pavilion growing higher with each passing moment, the strength in his legs going turning to mush as the excitement grew.

"Do you think the King will come?" asked a woman with a nasally older voice somewhere behind him.

"What do you think, you old hag? He hasn't left that damn castle of his in years. I doubt a few wild animals and a traveling train of freaks is going to arouse him from within those cold walls," a man answered, his voice gruff.

"It's a pity he has himself locked up there like he does. A wife's death is hard…"

"You mean the Queen's death," the man interjected.

"Yes, yes. The Queen's death was hard on all the kingdom, but it still isn't right. He has had all the time to heal, now he has to remember his people and this city."

Levi tried to look back, see who was talking in the ocean of heads that he seemed to only reach the shoulders of, but hands again found the middle of his back and pushed him forward.

"He's the king, and that is all there is to it. He'll do as he damn well pleases, regardless of what you old witches think."

"Watch your…"

The woman said in retort, but Levi lost the conversation as the wall of bodies in front of him split, and the dark entrance to the circus tent reared its opened mouth directly before him.

"Ticket please," said a deep booming voice.

Levi looked up and felt his blood go cold. The man was large, probably the largest he had ever seen. The sun was directly behind his ginormous round head, leaving his skin as dark as night, though looking at the bulging muscles of his forearms that were now crossed over a belly large enough for Levi to crawl into, his complexion was just as dark without the shade of the sun. White pearly eyes and yellow teeth larger than the nails on Levi's hands smiled down at him, waiting as the sounds of the crowd behind had already begun to grow unruly.

"Ticket please, my little prince," deep and thunderous as his voice was, his words were soft.

"I … I don't have one. I didn't know we needed one," Levi said as he searched the lining of his pockets, though he knew there was nothing there.

The man's eyes narrowed, and his lips straightened with his tightening face.

"What's the holdup?"

"If he doesn't have a ticket, throw him out of line!"

Calls were made by those still waiting to get in, and a few additional agreeing shouts were quickly becoming chants.

"Marco the Magnificent's show is not cheap, nor is it free. If you do not have a ticket, then you will have to step out of line," the dark-skinned man said.

"Where do I…" Levi began to say before he was shoved out of the line, his feet tripping over the dry cobblestone and sending him to the dusty ground.

"He doesn't have the money anyway. Look at him, he barely looks like he bathes," said a man dressed in freshly pressed pants and an impeccably white shirt.

Levi could see the pencil lead smeared behind the man's ear and the tape measure in his back pocket, easy pickings if it was of any value. He was a tailor, and with a second look, Levi recognized him. Ugene Hodings, a tailor from Merchant's way. Not exactly the best one in town, but still had enough business to keep him off the streets. Levi had stolen a few knives and scissors before from his shop, barely enough to get him a few slices of old bread, and not worth the half day run from the city guards.

"I bathe!" Levi yelled back, though the only one who gave him even a second look was the monstrous ticket man.

For a moment Levi watched as the line continued to file past and into the tent. Women, and men, children and old all handing little green tickets before being allowed to enter. Was he the only one who didn't have one? Where would he get a ticket and how much would it cost? He knew he still had a few coppers he could spare. Even his hard-earned tin bundled up under the king's road bridge would be worth it, but that was for emergencies and food. Wasn't this an emergency? What would it mean to be the only person in the entire kingdom who didn't get to see the circus?

Defeated, he turned and shoved his small hands into his empty pockets. Stupid circus. It couldn't be that exciting anyway. The King himself wasn't attending. Levi continued to lie to himself as he turned down the alley that led into the shadows behind the circus instead of away and back into the city.

* * *

"Grab the chickens and get your asses moving!" yelled out a man with a funny hat.

It had one of those flat tops, and it was almost half as tall as he was and narrow from top to bottom.

Levi sat up on the cobblestone wall that followed the King's Road as it rose toward the castle at the center of the city. His legs dangled over the edge, and he wiggled his toes at the sand and dirt that clung to them. His body was hidden in the shadow that stretched for what seemed like half the world behind the tent, the shade a cool reprieve from what turned into another scorching summer afternoon. He watched as the tall man, as thin as a bean pole and just as brightly colored in yellows and reds, barked orders and clapped his hands together faster to speed up the work.

There was a second entrance to the circus tent, more like a cut in the red fabric where circus members carried supplies in and out as the show continued. Mostly food and props, he watched as able-bodied men, rippling with muscles, their bodies painted in various colors, and their tight pants decorated with bird feathers moved with purpose, grabbing full crates and dropping off the empties. Hazy orange light beamed from the hole in the fabric as the tall man held it open like a father ushering his children in, a look of disdain on his face as the men hurried with their cargo and they pushed their way through.

Disappointment darkened his afternoon as Levi sat and listened to the show from the outside. The cheering of the crowd, the roaring of the animals, and music that ebbed and flowed with the excitement that he was missing out on. He hadn't seen a single person move along the road, either the King's Road or any of the side streets since the last person shuffled their way beneath the tent. His only visitors were the city guards who stopped to listen to the show themselves. A few stray cats meowed for food, and when he didn't have any, made their way down to the Circus' supplies, only to be shooed away the next time the man with the tall hat opened the tarp.

What was he going to do?

Everyone was in there, but he was out here. Why was it always him that had to go without? What did he do in a previous life that he'd be forced to live this one as a useless street boy? Maybe if he went back to the bridge, he could get the money and pay for a ticket. The show didn't sound like it was ending soon, but that money was all that he had, and he had saved it for an emergency.

Wasn't this an emergency?

He was alone in an empty city, the only soul left in this world, the rest swallowed by the magnificent world of Marco and his treasure of wonders.

The tent opening swayed as a warm, gritty breeze wrapped itself around the back of the circus. Levi could feel the sand in the air as it scratched at his skin and crunched between his teeth no matter how much he tried to breathe through his nose.

"I wonder if anyone is watching," Levi thought to himself out loud.

Looking up and down the street, nothing had changed. The last guard had continued up the King's Road an hour ago, and he didn't expect another for a long time. Grinding his teeth, Levi pushed himself to his feet and crouched as he walked down the descending road and tried to keep himself in the shade.

Eyes watching in all directions, he crept his way around the edge of the wall and slipped along the stone as it rose above him, leaving him in shadow as the gigantic tent towered over him. Cages rattled, and birds squawked as he closed the distance between him and the circus, his breath held while he tried to keep supplies between him and the entrance.

SQUAWK!

A duck jumped up and flapped dark blue tipped wings in its cage when Levi stepped next to it, feathers lifting into the air. Levi jumped back and hid with his back against the wall, his heart racing with his eyes locked on the tent. The tarp continued to wave in the afternoon air, but no one opened it. He could hear the cheering of the crowd and a man's voice directing the action within. It was deep and strong, commanding attention with every word and captivating in its endless story.

Levi couldn't stand being left out another minute. He looked at the duck, its deep brown eyes staring at him before he pushed himself to stand.

"Stupid duck, what do they need a duck around her for?"

He wiped the dust off of his pants, wiped a hand through his greasy hair, and tried to smear the grease off of his arm with the rear of his legs. He didn't want to stick out as a street kid. If he were quiet enough and stayed out of everyone's way, they'd never even notice he was there.

Steadying himself with a breath, he took a step away from the cages and boxes of supplies and approached the opened tent. There was no sound from anyone inside, no shadows along the floor to tell him they were waiting inside. What if there was? Where would he go? He took a final look up the road and found it just as empty as it had been. He was fast, faster than any other boy on the street. If they found him or said anything, he'd make it back to the door and lose them in the city. Very few knew the streets as well as he did. They were his home.

The red cloth was heavy and rough between his figures as he pulled it open and stepped into the tent. The light from inside was blinding, forcing him to squint to see anything, and the sound from within the area was deafening. Between the screams from the audience and the jovial chorus of the band, Levi could barely hear himself think. He could feel waves of sound pressing against his ears, a crackling that varied with the intensity.

Eyes adjusted, he let the circus canvas fall and began to make his way toward the noise. His heart raced with excitement and fear. He only had to get to the crowd. They'd never know where he came from then.

"You get those last two crates of Rock Ball Pins?" the man with the tall hat's voice called out.

Levi stopped mid-step. He couldn't be sure if they were talking to him or someone else. Oh, he prayed it would be someone else.

"Are you going to answer me or just stand there frozen? Did you get those last two crates or am I going to be stuck sending someone else?"

The man's voice was closer. He could feel his shadow creeping up on him, like a giant monster as the darkness widened and that tall hat of his stretched along the walls for as far as Levi could see.

Frozen with fear, Levi didn't answer. He couldn't if he had wanted to. His heart had stopped, his throat was as dry as the desert, and his strength was draining.

He wanted to fall to the ground. It took everything he had to not stand there and shake like a rattle.

"Look, I'm not gonna ask you again," tall hat said.

A heavy hand fell on Levi's shoulder, the digits strong and thick as they gripped down to the bone. A pinching pain lanced through his chest and jump-started Levi's heart. Without thinking, without considering his actions at all, the little street boy turned half a shoulder and looked at the man in his eyes. Deep and brown, the recognition that Levi wasn't a circus worker flashed like a lightning bolt through the man's features. Before he could get a firmer grip, Levi stomped his foot down on the man's shiny black boot.

The material didn't give much, though he had thrust his leg as hard as he could, it was enough to loosen the man's grip. A tug of his shirt and Levi was free, but he didn't run for the tent's unblocked exit. He turned and raced for the show. He didn't know why; he didn't think about it. Protests and calls for help were lost as the distance between him, and his chaser increased, and the space between the show and his flying feet decreased.

His breaths came in gulps as he continued around the fabric-created corridor. Light from the center flickered as the cloth walls rippled with the sound of the audience, its cheering now as loud as thunder and the heat of a thousand bodies warming the air as Levi ran for his life. He couldn't tell if he was being chased, the pounding of countless feet and the roar of an animal he had never heard rang in his ears as he continued to keep one foot in front of another.

"Ladies and gentlemen, for a feat you have never witnessed before in your lives," the announcer who must have been Marco called out.

Levi could hear his words, his strong voice briefly taking away any thought of his pursuit as the lights from the center stage opened. With a squint, Levi could see he had only a short distance before he reached the rows and rows of seated people. Everyone sat on wooden benches. Each new row was a row height higher until the last level had the people with their heads up in the fabric.

He had never seen this type of arrangement before, but he didn't have time to waste and look at it. A warm breath ran down the back of his neck, whether real or imagined, he didn't want to find out. The wooden framework of the seating created a skeleton that forced him to slow, he was small, and he was quick, but there was no easy way getting through the rib cage of this structure. At least the tall man would be too large to fit through as easily as he did.

"There he is, get him!" the man called out.

Levi turned to look. Dark shadows of the cloth tunnel billowing behind him, he pointed at Levi as six men stepped into view, their deeply tanned skin a contrast to the bright and vivid colors of the Tall Hat and his attire.

A shriek slipped from Levi's lips as he bolted between the frames as fast as he could. The men aiding in his pursuit were fast and well-muscled, their skin pulled tight against their frame. The part that scared Levi the most was they were small. Barely as tall as he was, they'd be on him at any moment.

Sweat ran down his face as he turned and ducked, stepped over and slammed his knees into the wood frames as he pressed forward. The pounding of the feet above him was an earthquake that shook the boards all around him and rained dust into his eyes. He could feel them getting closer. He wanted to look, but he feared they would grab him if he tried.

"Now, if you would all turn your attention to the center of the stage as Bullentiene the Hardheaded will now place himself into," Marco called out.

Levi shook his head. There was no time to get lost in what was happening. Maybe if he could make his way to the front, he could get out through the main entrance. There would be no reason for them to keep chasing him. He didn't even stay. He never even got to see a single act!

"Got you now!" a deep growl rolled as a hand like a viper's teeth snatched at Levi's collar.

The grip was tight, and the sudden jerk of his shirt sent Levi into a spin as the cloth tore. Crashing to the ground, he could see three of the men climbing out from underneath the audience, dark smiles on their faces and their eyes bright with the hunt.

"Please, I just wanted to," Levi pleaded.

BOOM!

An explosion rocked the tent. The ground shifted under their feet and unbalanced the three men who had gotten within an arm's length of him. Back peddling and turning, Levi pushed himself back up and into a run as his ears rang like a siren.

What was that?

It no longer mattered. It had given him a few

more seconds to get ahead.

"I told you; I will not go out after Bullentiene! The air is full of smoke, and the damn audience is too stunned to truly appreciate my show!" a woman's voice yelled.

At least Levi assumed she was yelling, the terrible pain in his ears was excruciating as the pounding of his blood thundered in his head.

Turning the corner, Levi never had a chance to stop as he plowed into a woman carrying a silver tray and an array of powders held in clay cups. White ivory silk flapped, and words Levi could only imagine cursed out as he and the woman tumbled over one another.

"What in the seven hells?" she started to say as she pushed herself off the ground.

"We've got you now, you little thief," one of Levi's pursuers said as his iron hands wrapped around Levi's arms. "You aren't getting away that easily."

"Please, I didn't steal anything," Levi pleaded. "Look, I don't even have anything on me."

Levi's heart raced. More than from the running, everyone was looking at him, their eyes burning holes right through his body.

"You sneaked into the tent through the back and intended to watch the show without paying for a ticket. That in the eyes of the law is called stealing." Tall Hat said as he appeared behind the ivory woman and the three men that now held Levi.

"No, you have it wrong, I do have money."

Everyone waited. Levi knew he could go get the coins, it would take all he had, but at least they couldn't arrest him.

"Your pockets are empty, and you're as dirty as the trash out back. Henry, have one of your performers go grab the city guard, there is too much of the show left to deal with this," the Lady in Ivory said.

Levi could feel the strength in his legs drain and tears ran down his cheeks. He only wanted to watch the show. Why couldn't he watch the show?

"What is going on here?" Marco's voice called out. Everyone stopped what they were doing. Even the men who held Levi stood straighter. "Any more noise out of you all and the audience wouldn't even be watching the show."

Levi's eyes widened as the large man turned the corner. He was big, broad-shouldered and his presence alone demanded their attention. Dark hair fell from a dark wide brimmed hat and a small beard framed his solid chin as he stood a head taller than everyone. Even Henry with his tall hat.

"Don't worry about it, Marco," Ivory said. "Henry found someone sneaking in. He'll take care of it, won't you, Henry?"

"Yes, ma'am," Henry said with a stutter.

"Let me see the thief," Marco said.

Levi's legs gave as the mountain of a man stepped forward with Ivory by his side. The only reason he wasn't on the ground was that his captors were too stiff to drop him.

"He doesn't look like much. How did he even get inside?"

Henry cleared his throat from behind everyone. He was now further away than he had been.

"Well, sir. Let me," he began.

"I know you," Levi said.

He didn't know why, and he couldn't even figure out where the strength came from, but the words flowed without his consent.

Marco turned back to him; a dark eyebrow lifted in question.

"You know me street thief? Everyone has heard of me and my traveling amusements."

"Oh no, sir," Levi squeaked out. "I mean, I know her." He pointed to Ivory with his chin. "I saw her enter the King's Palace back in the spring. She came by herself in a coach and fell into a puddle. She used curse words I'd never heard from a lady before. then she was ushered inside like a secret in the night."

"You're just confused, and a liar," Ivory responded before turning to walk away. "I've never been in the palace. Now, Henry, get him out of here."

"Wait, no! Please don't call the guards, I can prove it!" Ivory stopped moving. "If I prove it, will you please not call the guards. I swear I won't watch the show. I'll come right back. Please!"

"He's lying. Marco, just get rid of the street trash. You have to be back out front any moment," she said.

Silence waited between them, though the roar of the crowd was as constant in the background as the wind.

"Silence, woman. I'm intrigued by what he has to say." Marco knelt until his face was level with Levi's. "If you can prove that she has seen the palace, I will forgive you. Go get whatever proof you claim to have. Be back by the end of the show. If you are not here,

I promise you the city guards will not stop until they find you."

No words left Levi's lips as he nodded his head in agreement. There was no arguing with Marco once he spoke. It was like a spell, his words a drug you could not turn away from. Feeling the pressure of the men's grip leave his arms, a tilt of Marco's head had Levi running out the front of the tent faster than he had ever run before.

* * *

Ten paces. That was all the man they called Parko would let him have. They were a half dozen city streets from the circus, and the streets were still empty. Vendor stalls were idle, empty carcasses void of goods except for the broken pieces and the quickly rotting fruits that sat busted and open to the heat of the summer. It left a sweet yet sour smell to the gritty air as they continued undisturbed along the side of the cobblestone way.

"Return before the end of today's performance."

Levi didn't know how much time that gave him, but every once and a while he would stop to look up and down the empty streets and Parko would get him moving with a grunt that said time was running out. They had made it down King's Road, left at Merchant's Street, and across several others before they finally reached the Minisville River bridge.

It spanned the open water with its double lane arched road, cobblestones dusty and worn from the thousands of carts that are pulled over after paying the mandatory city toll for both merchants and pedestrians.

Levi would spend many a day watching as the merchants and farmers pulled tired animals across the river's expanse, sweat dripping from their faces and goods rattling from carts as the tires turned over uneven rocks.

Many an afternoon was spent following those carts, picking a fallen piece here or slipping a morsel into an open pocket as the traffic of carts and animals got held up before turning up Merchant's Road for the daily market.

"The sun is only a feather above the horizon, street thief," Parko called out. He stopped following and crossed his arms over his chest, the knots of muscles bunching and stretching his sun-leathered skin. "Marco has given us specific instructions to return, and we will be soon turning back around."

"We are almost there, I promise. It is right around the corner."

Levi skipped ahead toward the bridge, but instead of following the dusty path up and toward the archway, he ducked into the shadows and followed broken stones that wobbled loosely against its foundation as he descended under the stonework until he was level with the river's churning water.

The stench of refuse and stale water was thick as the humidity rose and stuck to their skin in the shadows of the bridge. Heat from the summer day struggled to push away the moisture that collected from the river, its water dark with runoff from the city's latrines, and the lakes that pooled in the mountains to the west of their city.

Curses and shifting stones followed him as Parko struggled to find footing down to the riverbank.

Most people didn't like going down so close to the water, its surface brown and oily as it slowed before turning south past the city and rolling deeper into the kingdom. This is what made it a home for Levi; stinky, dirty, and full of waste, but no one bothered him down here. He climbed a few rocks up off the bank until he reached the arching stone above.

He never allowed himself to get too close to the river. Always afraid of falling in and being carried away, he made sure his home was always dry and up in the stonework as far as he could push it.

"You live down here, little thief?" Parko asked before wiping the back of his hand against his nose.

Levi could see water collecting at the corner of the man's eyes, the stench was something people always struggled with.

"There are very few places to choose from for a person like me. I'm safe here, for the most part. Guards don't bother me, and the other street kids don't want it," Levi said as he poked his head out from behind a few wooden crates he had 'borrowed' to create a wall to further hide his presence. "Who said I was a thief? I only borrow what I fully intend to return, unless it is food. A boy has to eat, doesn't he? I don't intend to die in these streets. One day I'll make something of myself."

He listened as the man chuckled under his breath before coughing at the smell. What he was looking for was hidden in the few possessions he had. Scrambling his hands over the goods, he pushed aside the broken pottery and leather belts and straps, items he intended to sell or barter with over the next few weeks before his store of dried meats and stale bread ran out. Which, with the rumble of his belly, reminded him was no more than a few days away.

Beneath it all sat the box. Made of thin beach wood, dark and stained from water, he pulled the treasure out from underneath everything, and he sat with his back against the rough stone of the bridge. Washed up along the bank, the box was one of the first things he had found the day he was banished down here, dirty and filled with gritty brown water, it was the most important yet useless thing that he owned. He ran his fingertips over the smoothed edges as he followed the stained lines with his eyes.

"Uh, huh," Parko coughed and started to walk closer.

"I almost have it," Levi called out with a quick look around the broken crates.

The man stopped a half dozen steps away, a look of annoyance on his tanned features before he turned back to the churning water below.

Pulling on the broken latch, the thin wood opened silently across his lap revealing the contents within. A small cloth pouch sat tied with a thread of catgut. Inside sat his life's savings. Two tins, six copper. Enough to buy him food for a week, maybe more if he bought only stuff that would store, but it was something. He intended to keep enough hidden until he had a gold piece. Then he'd get himself a real home, somewhere that didn't stink of waste and wasn't flooded every fall when the rains returned.

Next to the nearly empty pouch sat a single slipper. Brown and crusty, the ivory shoe had not aged well beneath the river, but it was still as it was when he had pulled it from that puddle. She had left it that day she entered the palace. Maybe she didn't remember, maybe it hadn't even mattered.

One thing was for certain in his mind. It was Ivory's shoe, and he would prove it to Marco. Something about the man scared him. His voice could demand the attention of an entire city, and if he said the guards would not stop until he was found, there wasn't a heartbeat in Levi's chest that believed those words weren't true.

Removing the shoe and closing the box, he replaced his most prized possession and buried it beneath his weekly collection once again.

"We can head back now," Levi called out.

Water splashed several times before he looked around the crates. Parko's arm was already reared back for another throw. With the ease of practiced skill, the rock splashed into the water and skipped a dozen times before sinking into the murky river.

"Good, Marco will already be waiting," Parko said.

Levi swallowed into a dry throat and led the way back up and away from his home and back to the tent.

* * *

Fire crackled on burning torches as Levi watched the citizens of the city file out. Among laughter and amazement, he could only get small bits of story about what had happened. Animals with teeth as tall as a man, cats with claws that could cut boards of wood in a single swipe. Images both scary and exhilarating flowed through his mind as the men and women, nobles and city merchants, moved like a single mass. Their departure slow for he imagined that none of them really wanted to leave.

"Is that all you have, little thief?" Parko asked, his arms crossed over his chest.

Levi looked at the filthy shoe in his hand. The expensive material wrinkled and compressed from months inside that sea wood box. He didn't answer, but he wondered if that was the only thing Parko could do, skip rocks and cross his arms. He looked formidable, his eyes as dark as an animal, but he had kept his distance, which was always several steps away.

"This will prove it was her. It is ivory just like her dress. You will see."

"There are a lot of ivory shoes in this world, and a lot of women," Parko replied before turning his eyes to a bird that flew overhead.

"I know it is her. I saw her that day, plus she had used words when she dropped this that I had never even imagined. Curses that made me cringe."

Parko turned back and smiled, but he didn't say anything.

"Marco will see you now," called out Henry, his tall hat as dark as night.

His bright colored clothes reflected the firelight in devilish reds and oranges.

"It is time, little thief."

"I'll show you one day I am not a thief."

Parko nodded his head and waited until Levi was following Henry before he continued behind him.

They didn't move to the front of the tent, a few members of the audience still standing around looking to see if they could catch another look at some of the wonders within. They moved into the darkness behind the tent, the shadows danced between the burning torches that followed up the rock wall that lined the King's Road, leaving the back entrance a dark hole in the deep red canvas.

"You better have what Marco is expecting. He is a lenient man, but he does not like those who waste his time," Henry said while he held the tent open, his eyes stern and lips creased into a tight line.

A thick, musty smell filled the air of the tent, warm and rich as Henry and Parko followed suit. Without saying a word, the tall beanpole of a man stepped in front and began to lead them toward the main stage, around the outside where he had been chased just a short time before.

The circus was quiet, everyone gone, and even the animals hushed wherever they were being held. Golden light blinked and swayed in the center of the giant ring, sand rustled and darkened where claws and boots had ground paths in the soft medium. Seating surrounded the entire arena, the highest points lost within shadow as Levi's eyes tried to adjust to the dozen or so new suns that burned around the circular pit.

"There he is, our guest of honor," Marco's voice called out from the darkness.

Levi's heart stopped before he looked around. Lost in the amazement of the circus, he hadn't noticed when Henry and Parko had left him and melted into the darkness. Where was everyone?

"Do you have the proof you claimed you could use against our sweet Mrs. Ivory, the queen of all women?"

Marco's voice was all around him, and he could feel his knees weaken. He wanted to run, hide in the shadows, though the deep voice said with no words there was nowhere for him to go.

"I have it right here," Levi's voice squeaked out.

He held out the shoe in front of him, his arms shaking and the filthy slipper nothing more than a piece of trash dirtying the gloriousness of the magnificent circus.

"A shoe? You desecrate the name of a beauty such as Mrs. Ivory for a shoe?" Marco's voice deepened and crackled in Levi's ears.

"She dropped it before entering the palace. She swore at the guard like nothing I had ever heard before. Well, until I heard her again today."

Laughter rolled through the empty arena, the echoes filling the room with voices. Cold sweat ran down Levi's back, and he almost dropped the shoe.

"Her mouth will one day get her in trouble, I always told her that," Marco said between laughter.

The large man stepped out of the shadows across the sand arena from Levi. He had removed his red coat and hat letting his dark hair fall down to his shoulders and his white shirt opened down to the middle of his chest. He took formidable steps as he cleared the distance between them in only a few strides, his smile stretching from ear to ear.

"If there is anyone who can curse like her, then I'll be a surprised man, and I'll tell you, my boy, there is very little that surprises me anymore. Ivory, get out here!"

Levi's heart hadn't restarted now that Marco was standing next to him, but he stiffened his legs so the circus master would not see him shaking. A cage slammed shut off in the distance before the white glow of ivory began to materialize out of the darkness to their left. Her dress shined like it had a light of its own, and her hips swayed as she glided across the sand. She was beautiful, her legs long and her face soft behind eyes that said she could eat you alive. Long brown hair swayed down to the middle of her back with every step.

"I'm telling you, Marco, this boy can't prove anything," she said in annoyance.

"Let's see if he can prove himself. What is it exactly that you have? I don't think you ever gave me your name."

"Levi, sir," Levi answered, his gaze going from Ivory to his dirty feet which sank partially into the sand.

"Well, Levi. Show us what you have."

Shaking in his hand, he lifted the ivory shoe.

"A dirty slipper?" Ivory chuckled before she waved the back of her hand and turned to walk away.

Marco remained silent.

"I saw you drop this in a puddle when you got out of your carriage. Then you entered the palace without retrieving it. I found it and have kept it till this day."

She didn't look back as she continued to walk away.

"Ivory."

She stopped where she was.

"Try on the shoe."

"Marco!"

"Do it now!"

The woman's shoulders slumped before she turned around. No longer gliding across the sand, she stomped her feet back to where they stood at the center and snatched the slipper from Levi's hands. Kneeling she removed a similar ivory slipper, one that was marked by nothing in anyway.

Levi watched as her pale tiny feet glided into the dirty slipper as if it was made for her foot and only her foot. Anger flashed in her eyes as she looked up at Levi, and a feeling of relief mixed with fear flooded through him.

"It looks like you forgot something when you were specifically instructed to never be seen entering the palace, Abigaile," Marco said.

Mrs. Ivory, Abigaile, looked up and her eyes changed from anger to sadness.

"I know, your highness. I came just as you instructed, as you always instructed. I have no idea how this little thief saw me. I swear, it won't ever happen again," she said as she dropped her eyes to the ground.

Levi swore Marco had swollen to twice his size, his shadow now enveloping her entire body. Your highness?

"It looks like this time it was only this little boy. Next time, it could be someone of greater importance. Now, get out of my sight. We'll talk about this later," Marco demanded.

With a nod, Abigaile pushed herself back to her feet and ran from the center stage.

"Now, Levi as you call yourself, what am I to do about you?"

"Please don't call the guards, your highness, I swear I didn't even see any of the show."

"The show?"

Levi stopped before the next plea could come out.

"Wait, your highness? You're the king!"

Without hesitating, Levi dropped to one knee.

"I'm so sorry, my king. I didn't know it was you. I swear I didn't know."

Levi waited for guards to charge out of the darkness and drag him to the prisons. Oh, only if he hadn't needed to see the circus so badly.

"Get up, my boy. No one knows who I am other than those of the palace and those within this show."

Using all the strength he could muster, Levi pushed himself to his feet.

"But why, sir?" Levi asked before he could stop himself.

"That is a good question, my boy, a really good question. But first, we have to answer a more pressing issue. What are we going to do about you and what you have now seen without a ticket?"

Levi swallowed hard as the king placed his hand on his shoulder and led him into the shadows.

* * *

"Everything looks different now, doesn't it?" Chapman asked.

Levi looked over at the older man. His beard was still a dirty gray, more white than dark, and it still dropped below his waist. All the hair and sun-dried wrinkles held a soft smile that relaxed Levi as the cart bounced over the cobblestones.

Behind him sat the single carriage, polished

ivory and simply adorned on the outside, it rode with little fanfare as they approached the Palace of the King of Kuronish. Inside sat Mrs. Ivory, only known as Abigaile to him and the rest of those he now called family within the wonders of Marco and his circus.

They had been traveling west, chasing the summer warmth since they left their home city, reluctant to stop until the cold hard winter returned. Levi had learned that after the king had lost his wife, he had suffered in mourning for a year wondering the halls of his dead palace, waiting for something, anything to show him what was next.

It wasn't until the day Abigaile, before she became known as Mrs. Ivory, petitioned for a merchant's ticket to perform her one-woman show daily on Merchant Street. Something about her, either in her eyes or how she had a glow that could light up the darkness had awoken a fire in the King that he had thought died with his queen.

He was a faithful man, one who swore that the only woman he would share his chamber with was the mother of his three sons. But he was also one who could not sit idle in the palace. Why would a woman so extraordinary be relegated to a single merchant table on a street where she would never be known? In her he saw an adventure, an opportunity to see the world, but not as a king. Moving from kingdom to kingdom as someone who brought excitement to the people, he lived a life where everything changed at a moment's notice.

How much his sons knew of his exploits, Levi did not know, nor did he dare to question. It appears he had discovered the secret unknowingly in the early spring when Abigaile was slipping into the palace to prepare the king for this year's rounds. Knowing that the king left the palace and the kingdom to the reign of his sons as he traveled with a circus of creatures and freaks was something that could have ended up putting Levi in the dungeons until he died of old age. Maybe it would have ended with his head rolling down King's Road, but to his amazement, their leader was a compassionate man.

To keep the secret, Levi now worked for the circus. He traveled as one of Mrs. Ivory's lookouts, watching for other street "thieves" who may spot the beautiful woman as she traveled and sets arrangements with Kings in their palaces unannounced to the nobles and peasants alike. It is a simple job for he gets to ride with Chapman a lot and his stable of horses, but it is a world better than sleeping under a bridge every night.

On his belt dangles a small coin pouch, tied together with a string of catgut that reminds him every day of where he came from. Inside, the same dirty coins bounce as the cart moves through the city streets, but they are not alone. A single ticket remains with him at all times, reminding him always what happens when you try to watch the show without a ticket.

The End

About the Author

William J. Seymour is the author of stories in various genres that include fantasy, horror, science fiction, and comedy. He lives with his family in Pennsylvania and looks forward to what the next story will bring.

Other Titles by William J. Seymour

Azhana Falls
Dark Choices
Dark Secrets

Traveling Merchant
Merchant
Pestilence

Christmas Scares
Trail of Darkness

All Titles Available at BookFurnaceBooks.com